Praise for

SLIME LIN

"A cult classic is born. Jake Maynard's inspiring *Slime Line* is a backward glance at what the American novel could achieve before it got highjacked by English departments. Stumbling through the stinking grist of the salmon-processing slums, written with fish-gut fingers, and fueled by an impetuous, chemical verve of prose a la Thom Jones, *Slime Line* exposes Alaska's wage-slave work camps via the addled observations of its indefatigable narrator, one Garrett Deaver, a kid wielding a fillet knife manically passionate about a job that will leave him beaten, abandoned, and hiding from the police inside a floating trailer park while still attempting to solve the mystery of his father's death. Sinclair and Steinbeck would applaud this novel's eye, but it's Maynard's outrageous characters loosed upon the Alaskan seacoast that propel *Slime Line* into page-turning madness. Maynard gets every word right."

— Lee Durkee, author of *The Last Taxi Driver*
and *Stalking Shakespeare.*

"Maynard's *Slime Line* is an arresting read that sinks its claws deep into your gut and dares you to blink. It's a story of hard work, loss, exploitation, and family set against a backdrop of blood, ice, and heavy machinery at an Alaskan fish-processing plant peopled by misfits, scoundrels, and ghosts. You'll never look at a salmon fillet the same way again."

— Kim Kelly, author of *Fight Like Hell: The Untold
History of American Labor*

"A bold and forceful and glorious book, like a beer bottle smashed to bits over your head, leaving you sticky with glass shards. Jake Maynard's *Slime Line* depicts the world how it really is, or one hard slice of it anyway: the puke-inducing Alaskan commercial fishing sector. You'll learn how to gut a salmon in one chapter, then how to lose a family in the next. In both cases, it's not pretty. ('Everything,' as Maynard tells it, 'comes out clean except for the heart.') This is an eviscerating read, at once improbably raw and real."

— Ben Purkert, author of *The Men Can't Be Saved*

"*Slime Line* is a deeply compelling novel. Maynard's energetic prose is as gritty and raw as Alaska itself."

—Callan Wink, author of *August*

"There aren't enough gross books about work. This is a story that hasn't yet been told, and thank goodness Maynard was in the right place to bear witness and tell it. *Slime Line* is a wild romp, both compelling and educational. It will change how people approach fish processing—and work, even—in Alaska."

—Brendan Jones, author of *The Alaskan Laundry*

"*Slime Line* is a stone-cold winner: a book about the dirty work of capitalism, searching for a missing father, and reckoning with your legacy. It's full of fish guts and lousy shifts, but it's also driven by a big, beating heart. I found it impossible to put down. As in all great books, the big catch here is the truth, and Jake Maynard hauls it in, one gorgeous sentence after another. Tender, musical, sad, funny as hell. Read it."

—Steve Almond, author of *All the Secrets of the World* and *Truth Is the Arrow, Mercy Is the Bow*

Slime
Line

A NOVEL

JAKE
MAYNARD

West Virginia University Press • Morgantown

Copyright © 2024 by Jake Maynard
All rights reserved
First edition published 2024 by West Virginia University Press
Printed in the United States of America

ISBN 978-1-959000-19-8 (paperback) / 978-1-959000-20-4 (ebook)

Library of Congress Cataloging-in-Publication Data

Names: Maynard, Jake, author.
Title: Slime line : a novel / Jake Maynard.
Description: First edition. | Morgantown : West Virginia University Press, 2024.
Identifiers: LCCN 2023043226 | ISBN 9781959000198 (paperback) |
    ISBN 9781959000204 (ebook)
Subjects: LCGFT: Satirical literature. | Novels.
Classification: LCC PS3613.A9576 S58 2024 | DDC 813/.6—dc23/eng/20231013
LC record available at https://lccn.loc.gov/2023043226

Cover and book design by Than Saffel / WVU Press
Cover image: Sport Fishing: Leaping Coho Salmon, 1950, American School (20th century)
Photo © GraphicaArtis/Bridgeman Images

The First Part

What do you call a fish with no eyes?

FSH.

The Klak Fancy Letter
Wednesday, June 7th

Hello! Hola! Nihao! Buna! Czesc! Halo!

Welcome to the Klak Fancy Salmon, LLC. This daily announcement will update you on important news at the processing facility. You will also get our fish counts and info about FISH 101 Bonuses. With the start of the 2006 salmon season just days away, the crew at Klak Fancy is busy making sure we're ready to have a safe—and profitable!!!—season.

Rules to Remember:

*You must be processing fish by the official start of your shift! The start time isn't the time that you clock in! The start time is the *latest possible time* that you can begin working. Therefore, you must clock in at least 9 minutes before your shift. If you clock in 5 minutes before your shift, you're late! When you're late, your pay is reduced by 15 minutes.

*Respect private property! This includes fishing vessels and all the homes in and around Klak. You can walk on the beach but steer clear of the tidal flats because **the mud can be dangerous.**

*Watch out for bears! We will only have a few hours of darkness each night, but be especially watchful at night.

*Conserve water and **limit your showers**! Once the season starts, you'll be too tired to shower, anyway. You might as well get used to it.

*Klak Fancy Salmon is alcohol-free. Cigarettes and international phone cards can be purchased at the company store, open during every break.

Fish Processed: 0 (But not for long, of course!)

Weather: High of 52, light rain. Sunrise—5:21 a.m. Sunset—11:30 p.m.

Alaska Word of the Day: Sockeye—The type of salmon you'll mostly process. Sockeye travel from the deep ocean through Bristol Bay each year to spawn. Last year, fishermen caught nearly 25 million sockeye in Bristol Bay.

One

The spring season's over and the herring are finished. We've squeezed out the eggs for a Japanese grocery store chain and flaked off the scales for some cosmetic company to grind into lip gloss. It made me feel good on the tired days to know someone, somewhere, was smearing my work on their lips. Maybe even a flake of my skin, a barb of hair, a drop of blood. The most important season of my tiny life hasn't even started, and who knows how much of me is already spread out across the world?

Honestly I'm not even sure where the *Excellent Fillets* and *Great Fillets* and *Very Good Fillets* ended up after we sorted and glazed and froze and shipped them. Someone's fridge, I guess. Yours? All the bonus parts—the bones and heads, the fins and flabby bits—that shit got swept into the chummer and ground into a slurry and baked into pet food at a plant down the road. Fishmeal's the industry term. We call it the gravy.

But now the chummer's steel lips are sealed. The vacuum sealers, the header and gutter, the power-knives, the propane-powered forklifts, stinking like a stomach bug—all of it shut down. Even the crew packed their shit and flew back to

Anchorage. Then Fairbanks, Seattle, Bogotá, Manila, wherever. Not me. Where else would I even go? They let me stick around and clean the cannery.

It's not actually a cannery—remember: flash-freezing preserves freshness!—but that's the word the old guys use. Processor's the most accurate. When I practice explaining it to people back home, I think of it like a fish factory. But that's not quite right either. It's the opposite, a factory in reverse. Fish are taken apart. Meat gets made that way. On disassembly lines.

That came to me yesterday when I was laying belly-up scrubbing a month's worth of pasty herring gunk from underneath a conveyor and a scale flicked off the brush and went so far up my nose I had to spit it out. There's no way to describe that smell so there's no point in trying.

If that gives you the icks you won't like it when the freezers get thawed out. There's six of them, box-truck-sized, and during the season fish and water and blood freeze on the floor, six inches thick. Yesterday I flipped the OFF switch and propped open the heavy doors. And now, right now, I'm shoveling out what's left. A million little mammoths in their own thawing permafrost.

Can you believe I used to be squeamish? I wouldn't even scrounge for quarters in the couch cushions because of the crumbs and pubes. The wet wads of hair in the shower drain used to make me sick. One time I yakked because of a dead deer in my dad's pickup. But disgust is a feeling you can swallow. Look at me, Exhibit A, ankle-deep in the goop. This yellow raingear with tiny scales stuck to my goggles. What would my dad think of me now? In the dull days he snaps at me. There's slobber hanging from his jaws. I smack his nose. I tell him to lift his leg someplace else. This is my life. This is my *me*. This is the world that was made for me.

There's no way else to explain it. Soon I'll be a salaried foreman at one of Alaska's premier sockeye salmon-processing facilities. Soon I'll be paying off my credit card. Soon I'll earn clipboards for hands and a megaphone throat. I'll get my own crew of cannery newbies, flown to Klak from around the world, passports and work visas mashed into their palms. They'll be so lost, poor little fuckers, just like I was, ogling at the spongy taiga, the staggered trees, the scrapped machines, the trailers, the hitchhikers walking through the rain, the alders with trash bags clinging like flags saying I-Give-Up, and those foreign kids might say in their own language, *this looks fuck-all like the brochure*.

So what. It's better. Klak Fancy Salmon, LLC. We produce first-rate, ethically sourced, wild-caught herring and salmon, just fucking dripping with heart-healthy omega-3s. And me? I'm Garrett Deaver and I'm twenty-two years old and I'm about to climb this ladder. Some people here call me Deaver the Beaver, or Beaver, or Beav, which are all fine, because just like a beaver, I am an industrious motherfucker.

The past—men were men were men, amen. My dad was a commercial fisherman but he gave me shit directions north. Then he dove off a balcony, split his head. That was almost three months ago but this is about me. And really, it's about fish in the way that everything here is about fish. Nobody'll tell me exactly when the salmon will show and even the scientists can't say how they make it from the Pacific. Supposedly some combo of sunlight, and the smell of their home streams floating way out in the ocean, and the magnetite in their skulls working like a compass. Magnetite! They got coordinates lodged in their peanut brains.

People keep telling me that, like it's some big moral.

TWO

For five days the Filipino foremen and I scrub the plant and then the good work's done. The Filipinos are old-school Alaskeros, processor pros. They got their own trailers, their own shower house. They hop from winter jobs out on the Aleutians to the bay in the spring, working as supervisors and driving forklifts. They're always telling me to chill. They're always laughing at the way I walk. Rest up, they keep saying, smug with experience. I'm sure it works for them. They don't know me at all.

I live in the bunkhouse, a low, scabbed-together tin building just behind the main plant. It's blue, or at least it used to be blue. Now it's rust. Inside, just rows of cots like an orphanage. It's empty now except for me and three Moldovans who showed up early for salmon season. Mostly they play cards and smoke until it's time to start drinking. There's no internet, one payphone, and beers at the bars in Klak cost more than we make in an hour of work. I've already thumbed through all the books I can find. I mix-and-match, flip to random pages, find spots where the stories overlap. Wild, the meaning you can make for yourself. Dean Koontz and the Bible. Tourist brochures and a self-published history of Bristol Bay. I'm studying up. It's important to know everything. What else is an industrious motherfucker to do? You can only sleep so much when the sun barely sets and the Moldovans sing American pop songs drunk in the middle of the night. "Lend to me, please, your fire machine," one of them said to me last night around midnight, poking me for a lighter over my surplus army blanket.

There's two types of routine—the kind that keeps you sane and the kind that makes you crazy. My eyes are wide open here. I got enough self-awareness to know that the processor for me is like an ointment. If I could, I'd bottle it and rub it on my chest in the downtimes. Who wouldn't pick sanity? While I wait for it, I wake up when the breeze funnels in with the high tide and rattles the bunkhouse's loose siding. Outside the gulls and ravens and endless twiggy-legged shorebirds are talking shit and some old truck's always idling. From the main plant near the gravel road from town, an easy slope runs down to the bunkhouse, and next to that there's a dozen singlewide trailers where they store gear in the winter and more workers in the summer. Then the shower house—a doublewide smacking of septic where mosquitos the size of hummingbirds are waiting to suck blood from your ass cheeks—and past that the chow house, where they lace every meal with bruised fish. After that, a low hump of dunes, just sand, and a few gravel paths that lead to the boatyard and the river.

It's June in Bristol Bay. All the chunks of river ice that passed by for the last month, groaning against the quay wall, those are finally over. The ground's thawed now too and maybe the cold mud would dry out a little if the sky would ever give it a chance. It's never raining hard but it's never *not* raining. Like even the weather has the preseason yips. In the boatyard, fishermen prep for the season. All the boats on the dry, packed into rows, propped upright with rigging and wooden blocks. They look like the fishermen before the season starts—vulnerable, exposed. Balls deep in debt. You should see those guys pacing around, tugging on their hair. Every little problem's a code red. The whole season teetering on having the boat ready for opening day. Captains screaming, deckhands hauling crates of canned food, sparks flying from last-minute welding jobs, saws sawing, rope and net everywhere. The air smells manic—bleach and brine, exhaust and last year's fish. Maybe that's what killed him. The stress, not the guilt. Sometimes I see his busted face laid overtop the guys I pass. One time he bought me a bright orange Huffy with four chrome pegs. He said, you learn some tricks before I get back. He said, I'll teach you how to patch a tube.

I was a flat-tire kind of kid. Never even knew which way to turn a wrench. Dad skills—every time I find a new one I flush with this deadly sort of embarrassment. Driving stick, that's a peak dad skill, one I forgot about until the captain of a boat called *The Matthew* offered me twenty bucks to drive a net up to the net lady, who mends the nets. *The Matthew*'s part of a little clique of boats called the God Squad. I get a lot of work from the God Squad because everyone hates them. Everybody hates them because they refused to strike for higher prices like a decade ago. Half the processors are sold now, most of the deckhands swapped out, even some of the boats are out of the game.

Supposedly people still slash their nets. Like this one. The God
Squad's truck doesn't have a muffler and only drives in reverse.
The driver's side door is spray-painted WWJD. The bench seat's
so tore up they just threw a canvas tarp overtop of it.

My old buddy Nick Destin tried to teach me to drive stick
but now, with the deckhands watching, the clutch pops and I
lurch backward and die. They're laughing now. What else is new?
This is good shit right here—some fucking pussy can't even drive
a stick. The feeling's always the same, like I've been turned inside
out and everybody can see all my organs, my bones, my limp
little heart. My pink meat sticking to the canvas tarp. Inside-Out
Boy! That's me. I unpeel myself and I start the truck up again, get
moving, overcorrect the wheel, get stuck in the soft sand, fanta-
size about killing myself, and let some deckhands push me back
onto the gravel.

The door to the shack is open and an old country record plays.
Some lonesome cowboy wailing like a hand's squeezing his
throat. The shack's made of scrapped boat parts, and it shows.
You can see the past life of every little thing. One of the windows
used to be a porthole and the walls are old deck planks, cracked
black and sticky with tar. The place is strung with Christmas
lights, winking out of time with the music. I rap my knuckles on
the glass, it rattles, I walk in.

"Is it for *The Matthew*?" she asks, not looking up from her
work. "I charge him double."

I say, "He said you'd try to screw him."

"I wouldn't fuck him with your dick."

"He said he needs it done today."

"You fishing for Christ?"

"Cannery."

"Cannery," she says. "I remember back when they actually canned fish."

"I'm reading a book about it," I tell her. "It must be rubbing off."

"That's the problem with books," she says.

Her name is Bonnie and she sits cross-legged on the plank floor with a section of net folded out in front of her. She's using a spool of twine to mend spots where a net's gridding has broken. Behind her, two camp chairs and a cardboard cutout of Elvis. Walls plastered with maritime bullshit: life rings, a captain's wheel, baleen, vertebrae of different sizes swinging from pieces of twine. On the windowsills are old wooden net buoys the size of a fist, all whittled into different shapes. Salmon. Bears. Boats. Faces with gull feathers for hair. What a wet dream for the attention deficient.

She's a small, messy woman with tight silver curls. She wears black overalls, all tore up from years of getting stepped on. She works real fast and calm, and when she talks it's the same way. Quick but not manic, like Go is just her natural state. I love to watch people work, to figure out who-they-are by seeing what-they-do. Because who are you and what do you do are really the same question. My old counselor, Richard Pritchard, PhD, told me that.

"So you're just, what, laboring for the God Squad?" she asks after a while. I'd been fidgeting with the animal bones next to the buoys.

"Yeah," I tell her. I set down the sharp bone I've been twiddling into my callouses.

"Possum cock," she says. "People used to use them for toothpicks."

"They said a week and we'll start seeing fish."

"It'll be two before there's enough to bother."

The wind blows the door hard against the shack. I open it again, prop it with a brick. You could know nothing about mending nets and still see how good she is at it. The way she works with her whole body, pinning the net with her knees, pulling it tight with one hand and winding the spindle of line through the gridding with the other, her old-ass fingers configured for one specific job.

I ask her how long's she been doing this and she says, "I saw Jefferson Airplane at a house party in San Francisco. I've been mending netting since shortly after that."

She looks at me. "White Rabbit?"

I shake my head. Never heard of it. The record ends and she jumps to her feet—she's still crazy spry—and flips it. I don't like music but yodeling at least sounds like labor. We unload the net and when it's stacked where she wants it, she says, "You know what, kiddo? I had a helper around here but she died."

I must be making a strange face because she's making a strange one back at me. Like there's wind in her eyes. I've got this fucked-up habit of smiling when I hear terrible news. I don't do it on purpose. The corners just pinch up. Mr. Pritchard used to call it an *involuntary response to embarrassment*. As treatment, he used to read me devastating newspaper headlines while I practiced demonstrating concern. Now sometimes I still frown when I see boldface type.

I tell her no shit, my dad recently died, too. It just comes out of me. Like a sneeze in an elevator. Humiliation and freedom all tangled up, and now she's looking hard at her boots and I'm worried I fucked up.

"Whoops," she says, sighing. "I was just being metaphorical. She went to California last fall and came back knocked up. Now she has a newborn and no time for me."

Focus on your face, Beaver—

Hijacked Jets Destroy Twin Towers

Deadliest Tsunami in World History

Beltway Sniper Terrorizes a Region

"Come tomorrow if you want work," she says. "You seem solid enough."

How could I say no? Look at this strong, old woman. Those fucked-up fingers, those earthworm veins. The thin pink scar on her sagging throat skin, some ancient surgery leftover. She looks a little like my mom. She's an answer for my stomach. I have this tendency to throw up lately if I don't have anything to do.

I say, "Absolutely. Abso-fucking-lutely."

Three

Listen. Yesterday I got a little too deep in my feelings aka bullshit. I see that. I know the stuff they say about millennials but I'm not your typical summer job jackoff. Work, life, food, fuck, jump—the essentials all have four letters so we can write them on our knuckles and never forget. I showed up early to prove it to Bonnie but she wasn't there. So I walked to the boneyard, where the cannery puts decommissioned equipment to rust. Skeletal hulls, seized-up engines, dead bulldozers, conveyor belts that'll never run again.

It really looks like a boneyard, like a tar pit where dinosaurs sunk. Back in herring season, when the snow was still blowing sideways, a dead beluga washed up at the edge of boneyard. Belugas, they said, take to the estuaries, the places where the salty and fresh mix, like the mouth of the river. It was maybe ten feet long and white as a tooth with a big squishy penile head. The body had started to bloat but the face had this innocent smile, super doofy, completely trusting, a dipshit even in death, which is probably why some crust punk from Seattle climbed on top of it for a picture. Right when the kid crossed his hands to tell us to Suck It, a rib gave way and one boot broke through, just like he was falling through a rotted floor. He was just stuck there gagging, dry heaving through the eruption of stink. We got some pictures before we pulled him out and that night in the bunkhouse we laughed until it felt dangerous. Not quite crazy but toes on the edge. That's a feeling worth living for.

Bonnie Kohle, that's her full name. We work side by side, mostly quiet, endless knots, rain or no rain. Occasional stories—she likes to talk shit. Everyone is wrong. Everyone is an asshole. An arrogant asshole. Each guy that walks by is somehow the biggest asshole who has ever walked. She says it ought to tell me all I need to know about Klak Fancy that no locals work here. She says it ought to tell me a lot that there are no Yup'ik folks working here either. They're across the river, doing their own thing, processing their own fish. She usually just gets townie girls to work for her. She doesn't get involved with greenhorn cannery kids. A bunch of Facebook frontiersmen. Little fuckers, all of us.

"But you're lucky," she says, pointing at me with a wooden mending needle, so worn it shines. "I've always been a sucker for men who frown with their eyes."

We're rolling out ten feet of net on the gravel road in front of the shack to check it for spots fish might slip through. She gives me a piece of wood carved into the shape of a salmon. "The average-sized salmon," she says, wiggling it through the air to make it swim. "A seven pounder. This here's the picket-fence salmon. The nine-to-five salmon." The nets get dropped into the shallow bay and left to bob in the current. Fish that are too small pass through and bigger fish bump into the net, turn around, and swim away. But sockeye swim halfway through and find themselves stuck just behind the gills. They struggle until the net slides underneath their gill plate and they're dunzo. Native people used to grind little holes into rocks to weight their nets, keep them upright in the water, just like a volleyball net, but now fishermen use steel beads. Two centuries of lead in between, she says, can't be good for anybody. Everyone's poisoned, everybody's doomed. Meet Bonnie Kohle. She's not too popular in Klak.

"That reminds me," she says. "What's the difference between a bucket of shit and a fisherman?"

"What?"

"The bucket."

For a week we mend nets and haul nets and do other stuff with nets. She works me hard and late and I love her for it. The bunkhouse fills with workers. The bay fills with boats, like silver beer cans bobbing in a pond. Then, with the season bearing down and mending jobs finished, we drive down to the beach so Bonnie can collect driftwood to burn. It ain't the Alaska from the Discovery Channel—nope, flat and scrubby and wasted, waste*land*, tiny trees, boat repair shops, bite-sized birds, mud— but it's good to get out for a while. After four miles we hit Klak, quick as a blink, then the road turns to sand and drops down the bluffs onto the beach.

Low tide, sun pinging the water. So bright it hurts. I collect the cleanest driftwood and she cuts it up with a little chainsaw that she handles like it's her call of the void. She has a trailer hitched to the back of the Subaru and we stack the wood until the tires bulge. When the work's done I walk the mud flats a quarter mile out, chasing the fresh stink of brine, and I can see past the bluffs, down to the place where the beach curves away, past the tin fish camps with chimneys all puking smoke, way out to the open ocean. It's gray now. Lead heavy, like February. The sun's circling low and harsh and somewhere far away there's Russia—so far west it's already tomorrow.

Tomorrow. The season. Coming at me slow, then all at once, and I can see my future riding it bareback. I'm walking back happy and sane, stomping through sea puddles and watching the tiny stranded fish scatter like billiard balls. They know who I am. They know how I hustle, and I watch them dart in silver flashes into a tangle of lost net wrapped around a branch. Wait. Wrapped around a bone. A thick yellow bone with strands of sinew still clinging. A bear's leg. There was one hanging above the maintenance building door. That one still had the lower leg and claws.

I hold it up to my own leg. It fits like a femur, like maybe I could be a bear. That'd be cool. Sleep through the winter, wake and fish and repeat. The bone's heavier than you'd think. Heavy as a weapon. A big fist-sized ball on one end. It reminds me of this moose skull my dad brought home. He wrapped it in a box for my mom and covered it with packing peanuts. She shook the box and asked if it was a toaster oven. He just sat there grinning, my dad, all muscle and mustache and jacked-up teeth. He had a little knife in his pocket but took so long fishing it out that mom just tore it open with her bare hands. I remember that. And this—she started yelling before I could even see inside. She stormed out into the yard and the whole trailer shook from the slammed door. I looked down into that box and started laughing and my dad started laughing. He held the skull in front of his face and pranced all around the house, barking orders in my mom's voice—*Goddammit, Duane. Get your feet off my coffee table! Garrett, empty the fucking ashtray like I told you to.*

In the end, she wouldn't even let me keep it.

Now there's a rotten marrow smell poisoning my hands. A milky yellow fluid leeching from a crack down the middle. When I hold it up to my face, a tiny snail sticks out its head from the crack and shakes two brown antennae at me. The antennae say the truth will set me free. People are always giving me unwanted advice so I say so long, new buddy, and I huck the bone and watch it fly, end-over-end, dark against the dull sun. It lands noiselessly and is gone.

"You ready?" she asks me when I get back to the car. I've rinsed my hands in three puddles but I can still smell it. We start up the road, the little engine sounding ragged. I say I found a bear bone but it smelled too bad to keep.

"How you figure?"

I try to describe it. But what's there to say? It was white, or maybe yellow, and it smelled like death's taint, and was tangled in a net.

"Doesn't sound like any bear bone I know."

I say, "Moose?"

She slaps her thigh, says she didn't think moose worked with nets.

I say no way.

"Who can say?" she says. "I didn't see it."

"Shouldn't we tell somebody? The cops or Coast Guard or something?"

"Tell them what? You found a random bone but you tossed it back?"

"You're fucking with me," I say.

"And dead is dead is dead," she says, casual, like some bullshit embroidered on a pillow.

"You're fucking with me."

She shrugs.

Dead is dead is dead. We drive back through the village of Klak. The boats on the dry, the stick houses with dogs chained in the mud. Flowers growing in buckets, rhubarb growing in old truck tires. Fireweed in the ditch like my mom's smeared nail polish. Some Yup'ik girls watching some Yup'ik boys jump their bikes from a wood ramp in a driveway. White guys tinkering with a four-wheeler, a few more standing around them, beers in hand, hats propped high on their heads, toeing the scattered empties, spitting, telling lies, drawn toward the work in that way men are always drawn toward other peoples' work. Sometimes I want to know the name of the person who'd found his body. What that must've felt like.

We pass the liquor store, aluminum sided. The tiny grocery store wearing the same aluminum siding. The tiny police station, its lone SUV parked out front. It's funny, a place so big and all the buildings are small. Even the brand-new prefab library, its WELCOME sign cut into the shape of a salmon. Bonnie rolls down her window when we pass the pet food plant, where we send the gravy.

"You smell that?" she says. "They must be cooking."

The Klak Fancy Letter
Wednesday, June 21st

Hello Valued Klakers,

Tomorrow our first significant tender of fish will arrive. **Because the first 4 hours of your shift are considered training, you will clock in after you have trained for 4 hours.** Your supervisor will explain more.

Important News:

*You must be processing fish by the official start time of your shift! The start time isn't the time that you clock in! The start time is the *latest possible time* that you can begin working. Therefore, you must clock in at least <u>9 minutes</u> before your shift.

*There have been some reports of workers **trespassing on nearby private property. Respect private property!**

*Please don't feed the foxes that you see around the processor grounds. I know they're cute, but foxes are known carriers of rabies!

*Klak Fancy Salmon is alcohol-free. Cigarettes can be purchased at the company store, open during every break.

*Laundry service will begin this week. Write your name on a garbage bag and place the bag in the black plastic tote outside of your bunkhouse. We are **not responsible** for lost or damaged laundry.

Fish Count: 0 (But not for long!)

Weather: High of 63, light rain. Sunrise—5:16 a.m. Sunset—11:40 p.m.

Alaska Word of the Day: Rabies—Rabies is a fatal but preventable virus. In Alaska, it is spread mostly through foxes but also through dogs and other animals. Rabies causes animals to foam at the mouth and **become unpredictable and aggressive!** Please don't interact with any of the foxes you see around the processor grounds.

Four

On the eve of the season the vibe is pure static, charged like a fleece blanket. If it ever got dark, you could probably see the sparks in the air. Newbie workers clopping in their new brown XTRATUF rubber boots. Blistered, lost, scared, big-eyed, alive. And me? Soon the work'll come. Soon I'll have no thoughts, which is a calming thought. Like a handful of sand. Like a lobotomy but with an hourly wage. In high school, I read *Hamlet*, okay? Keeping busy is the moral. Would I trust my father's ghost to give me the details of his life? Can the leg bone name its owner?

Did I just find a body part on the fucking beach?

The answer to every question is fish.

A fish answers every question with *blub*.

I'm back at the processor with that stink still on my hands and the thought of that femur circling my head like cartoon stars, and I'm fighting off a freak-out when my supervisor, Helen, catches me and says to meet her at the chow house to help with orientation. She says another planeload of workers just got in and they need help with paperwork. She says just two days until we'll start seeing fish and I imagine myself filling up with sand, keeping me planted, just like Mr. Pritchard taught me to do.

Helen has high cheek bones and a blunt nose and skin that turns grapefruit pink in the freezers. She always wears a black hoodie and black jeans and a pale-yellow beanie so greasy it shines. Things always dangle from Helen's belt. A flashlight, a multi-tool, extra gloves, an intercom. Her belt's why the other foremen call her Batbitch, but I'd never call her that. Helen's beautiful and fierce. Someday I'll try to take her job, but for now I follow behind her to the chow house. As we walk, she tells me this summer we got workers from twenty-two countries. There's probably no place else in America where college kids and ex-cons bunk next to each other, and nowhere else on Earth where those Americans bunk next to Moldovans and Ukrainians and Poles and Russians and Slovenians. The Colombians and Brazil-ians and Mexicans are all put in trailers behind the bunkhouse. The Turks get their own trailer too, separate from the Eastern Europeans because they don't always get along.

"Politics," she says. "Everywhere you go!"

"I need your help," I say. "Something really weird just hap-pened to me."

She says if it's not about opening day it'll have to wait.

Inside the chow house the newbies are sitting on the long wooden benches, summer camp style, staring slack jawed at the paperwork in front of them. A few are already wearing their raingear and boots just in case a fish leaps out at them. Helen climbs up onto a picnic table near the broken soda machine in the corner, puts two fingers into her mouth, and whistles so loud a few newbies jump.

"We'll get back to your paperwork in a second," she says. "But first let me talk about some things." She goes on to explain the payment system with the sad enthusiasm of a DARE instructor. The base rate's $7.15 an hour for the first forty, minimum wage, then time and a half for each hour after that, up to about ninety-six hours a week. On top of that are the FISH 101 bonuses. If the plant processes 101,000 pounds of fish during your shift, you get an extra fifty bucks and the supervisors get an extra three hundred. As she talks, you can see the newbies straining at their mental math. "Are you ready to make some money?" Helen hollers.

"Yes," the newbies say.

"Louder if you mean it!"

"Yes," only a little louder.

"Look at Beaver here," she says, and they all turn to me. "Two months ago he was sitting on a bench like you, trying to remember his phone number. Scared shitless. And look at him now. He got a raise, got bumped up to a new job in the freezers."

LOOK—what a beautiful word. Those fat O's like eyes, gawking. Look at Beaver, here. She could say that all day and never once annoy me.

Look,

Look,

Look at him.

It's like cosmetology school—two months in, I'm the senior. I'm a person of consequence. When Helen's done and I make my rounds, helping fudge paperwork for foreign kids without the right documents, the newbies whisper questions to me about processing work.

"Will we work very hard?"

"Will we make good money?"

"Will there be many fishes soon?"

"Where nearby can you buy a MacBook?"

I try to give them the gist of it. Bad food. Long hours. Socks so hardened by sweat they stand up on their own. The cold concrete floor, the fluorescent buzz, the fish scales wedged under your fingernails that ooze pus. Sand-heavy muscles, sweet, sweet repetition, numbing your brain like a lab-engineered pill. And the money? You heard Helen. The bonuses will come. Just worry about kicking ass and getting shit done. I say this is my mantra and you can use it too.

I'm helping a table of college students from Bogotá when the door to the chow house slams shut so hard it blows a bunch of papers off the Turkish table. You can tell they're agitated by the way they're pointing fingers at each other, voices ticking up, someone just left. Helen and I lock eyes and she nods her head, telling me to go check it out.

Outside on the wooden deck where we take our breaks, one of the new Turks is pacing in his shiny brown boots. He's wearing a white hoodie that says OH YEAH! in acid green font. He's swatting hopelessly at the black flies above his head like a thought bubble. Even his cigarette smoke won't keep them away.

I tell him that nobody said he could take a smoke break yet, but he just stares.

"English?"

He nods his head yes and the flies take on the shape of a question mark. The sun's out again, and the gulls above us are shrieking at a raven, moving like a dark thought over the processor grounds. "I'm Bayram," he says, looking up at the birds. He's got one brown eye and the other one is blue, like a peacock feather.

He says, "I didn't know I was being paid for this."

"You can smoke all you want when you're done with your paperwork."

He says, "We're fools, yeah? I talked six friends into coming with me, and they are already angry with me."

Sure, I admit, it doesn't look like the brochure.

He uses the ember of one smoke to light another one. He snubs the butt on the deck and leaves it, watching while I bend over and pick it up. He says, "Nine hundred dollars on the flight, four hundred dollars to the recruiter in Ankara. One hundred and twenty dollars for these boots I will never wear again. Buy the rain jacket, buy the gloves, buy the phone card. Buy, buy, buy!"

From his hoodie pocket he pulls out a pack of cigarettes and starts waving them in my face, saying they cost seven bucks at the processor store. "Seven dollars!" he cries. "These are two dollars in Turkey." He's got a spasm on the eyelid of his blue eye now, fluttering like it's trying to fly away. Like even his face is feeling the fight or flight.

Helen's pep talks come to me. Then Mr. Pritchard's. My mom's numerology bullshit. None of them seem to fit. I say, "I put my last two years of college tuition on a credit card. If I thought this was a scam, I wouldn't be here."

Now my hand is sticking out, waiting for his. "I'm Beaver," I tell him.

"Like the animal?"

"Yes."

Five

When the paperwork's done, I hitch a ride to Klak in the bed of a Chevy pickup so rusty I can see the dirt road passing through the holes between my feet. I watch the dust rising and occasional bits of trash zip by. The Chevy hits a bump and a baseball-sized piece of the truck bed falls into the frame and is gone. I watch it shrink on the road behind us. I slap the side of the truck, ask to be let out. I say, "I think your truck's rusting out."

The guy says, "No fucking shit," and drives off, spitting gravel at me.

Klak's got one processor other than ours, Neptune. There's about five hundred workers glazing fillets and canning B-Grade salmon like they used to do in the old days. Neptune pays the same as us, smells worse, and their bunkhouses are so small you share a bed with two other workers, sleeping in shifts. The fish that don't make the cut at our plant or Neptune go to the fishmeal plant that hires mostly locals, Native and white, at twelve bucks an hour. People are always comparing bad smells to farts, but the place where they bake the fishmeal really, truly smells like farts. It smells like nothing other than farts.

It somehow smells like every kind of fart at once, but only farts. Nothing else. It's so bad they agreed with the town of Klak to only bake the fishmeal at night.

Past Neptune is the police station, just an outpost of the bigger station thirteen miles down the road in Paulson. It's about the size of a shipping container and the heavy steel door is locked. A sign says, CALL 911 FOR EMERGENCIES. Is this an emergency? My dad was dead for a week before I even found out. I can see past the bluffs from here. The bone's probably under a hundred feet of water by now. And my phone doesn't work here. I scribble a note on the back of a ruined employment form from earlier.

EMPLOYEE AT KLAK FANCY SALMON FOUND WEIRD BONE ON BEACH AT LOW TIDE NEAR HALIBUT POINT TANGLED IN FISHING NET THOUGHT MAYBE HUMAN LEG IDK PROBABLY NOTHING THOUGHT U SHOULD KNOW LEFT BONE IN FLATS LIKE AN IDIOT.

I tuck the note under the door and head to the Black Dog. Inside it's like a beachcomber's coffin, the usual coastal shit on the plywood walls. On the wall behind the bar are about a hundred portraits of boat wrecks. Boats upside-down. Boats teetering on rocks. Two boats on fire, and one small gillnetter partially sunk after two sea lions climbed aboard to fuck.

With the fishermen heading out, the Black Dog's empty. Just a Native guy on break from the fishmeal plant, smelling worse than my hands, eating chicken tenders and drinking Pepsi. At the other end of the bar, an old, sunburned drunk is swaying with a hand-rolled cigarette in his mouth. There's no bartender.

He turns to me and stares. "How're your dogs?"

"I don't have any dogs."

"Thought you were somebody else."

"Is there a bartender?"

He yells, "bartender!" three times in a row.

Fishmeal says that the bartender had to run out for cigarettes. I lean over the bar and grab a mug.

"Not sure if I'd do that."

I pour myself one and drink until the foam blots the tip of my nose. The drunk has a big mole on his forehead and when he squints the mole looks like it might take off and orbit his face. He asks me where I'm from.

"Pennsylvania."

"I knew a guy from West Virginia. Linus Smith."

I lean over the bar to refill my mug.

"That old pigfucker, Linus," he says. He pulls back his vest and before I can even see it, the glint says gun. "He's the reason I keep this on me."

I say what you're supposed to say. "Well that sounds like a story."

His name is Bill and in the mid-1970s he was living in the Alaskan interior and working as a hunting guide in the fall and a trapper in the winter. Linus lived in an A-frame in Talkeetna and was known for being generally full of shit. They knew each other because Bill's sister Jeanine and Linus had dated. One time Bill lent Linus his car and got it back wrecked with a note for Bill that read, "Got u some meat." There were two moose haunches lying in trash bags in the back seat. To say thanks, Bill kicked in the door to Linus's cabin, blew a few holes in the roof, and stole his good boots.

Bill stares forward as he talks. It's hard to tell if he knows that he's talking to a flesh and blood person. I pull myself another beer. I start to smell the bone on my hands again. Sometimes when I drink, things end up really weird.

"Listen," Bill says, and the mole starts bouncing from one side of his face to the other. That summer, Bill's sister Jeanine sent a letter, telling him that Linus was in Minnesota and the two of them were back together. The handwriting seemed off. He called her up. Jeanine couldn't be reached and nobody knew why. Bill flew to Minneapolis. His brother picked him up. It was snowing wet stick-to-your-eyelashes flakes and they drove to the town where Jeanine and Linus were supposedly living. They found the trailer where they lived and peeked in the window and saw Jeanine in the trailer's back bedroom with the door closed and bunch of dirty plates and dishes stacked around her. Her arm was in a sling.

Bill knocked on the door and Linus cracked it, looking strung out. Bill said he wasn't there to get into no kind of argument and lifted his palms upward like he was trying to catch the snow. Bill said that they were looking for Jeanine because their mother was sick. Linus said he hadn't seen her in a few days after they'd gotten into an argument. Bill produced a pocket bottle and swigged and Linus swigged and swigged again. Bill pretended to gulp while tonguing the bottle closed. He handed it back to Linus and told him he could polish it off. Linus wouldn't let him in the house.

"Well," Bill told him. "I better find my sister." He took a couple of steps off the porch and stopped. "Do you want to come along and help me check the bars?"

When Linus stepped from the door, Bill's brother cracked him upside his head with an axe handle then proceeded to beat him across the back with it. Bill also took a turn. They tied him to the sink and left with their sister, taking three hundred dollars in cash as compensation for pain and suffering.

"Not three years later," Bill tells me, "and that man went to prison for murdering a guy with lawn darts."

"Horseshoes," Fishmeal interjects. "You told me he beat a man to death with some horseshoes over a game of horseshoes."

"No, he killed him with lawn darts over a game of lawn darts."

They start to bicker, and Fishmeal throws his hands up and heads for the bathroom. I look at those two sea lions fucking and the broken boat next to them and I think about how my dad could've ended up like Bill, or like Linus, or like the guy drowned in his own net, and I think how I might've never known anything about him if his body hadn't crashed back through the roof of my life, and now, the awful power of my mind left alone, I see him in one of those photos, on some rocks. Ha! Uncanny! The shit I get into when I drink! But now the dream of falling forward. The drunken momentum of memories. I'm nodding off in class, I'm nodding off on the slime line, I'm not so much moving as being carried from the barstool, through the swinging half-door, behind the bar, past the beer taps, past the cash register. In the photo, he's older and fatter and bearded. Dad/not dad. He's wearing raingear and the picture is water stained and grainy. I turn to the drunk and say, "Hey did you know this guy?"

"You shouldn't be back there."

"Him." I point.

"Really, you shouldn't."

Now I'm shoving it in his face. "This guy. This fucking guy right here."

His eyes are crossed and he's trying to make sense of it.

"Yep," he says. "Joe. I heard he fell off something and died."

"Duane," I say. "His name was Duane."

"No," he says. "Pretty sure that's Joe." But before I can ask anything else, the door from the kitchen crashes open and I'm getting laid upside the head with some sort of club and the bartender is screaming at me and my father's picture hits the floor and breaks. I keep trying to explain but she keeps swinging and screaming THIEF and there are packs of cigarettes everywhere and bottles breaking and why are all the women in this state so fucking strong? I got ahold of the club and now she's kicking my shins and there's a hot liquid on my cheek and then the sound like getting slapped in both ears.

The old drunk's holding the gun, smoke in the air. A chip of plywood falls from the hole he put in the ceiling. He looks at the gun with a face full of surprise. An innocent, stupid face. The face of the dead whale. The bartender screams, "What in the fuck did you do that for?" and as they face off to argue about it, I bolt out the kitchen door into the gravel lot.

Six

I'm hiding out in a patch of alder between Klak and the cannery.

I ran as far as the hill outside of town but my boots were heavy and my head was spinning and my lungs started to burn, so when I was sure no one was behind me, I fell into the kind of slow, slacker walk that you'd expect from a cannery worker heading back from town. Because of the blood on my face, I didn't try to hitch a ride. Maybe that was a mistake because when I heard the police siren, I had nowhere to go but the ditch. I laid face down in the mud with the beer cans and packing peanuts and tetanus-spreading car parts while the cop SUV sped by. Then I climbed Rambo-style through a sluice pipe under the road, just wider than my shoulders, just high enough to keep my face above the mud, and I followed the drainage into the alders. I felt like a soldier, and I liked that. The purpose of it, the clarity of escape.

The bartender cut me with her club and there's a knot on my forehead like a horn is trying to sprout. It's starting to rain. You make your bed and you lie in it—my mom used to always tell me that. So this's my bed, down here in the ditch with all the other trash. This was never supposed to be a track-down-your-dad type of thing. I swear it. Alaska's a big place, and I just took the first job that accepted me. It was more about the vibes, the scene, the way the air smelled and the light moved. Like this thing Mr. Pritchard used to say—to tell someone about yourself, tell them where you're from. I've been thinking about that a lot since my dad died. Where was he really *from*? What place did he call his own? I know he came to Alaska for the first time in 1981, before he met my mom. I've seen the pictures of him then, all muscle and hair. He was twenty-two and laid off from a petrochemical plant in Pennsylvania. Why he picked Alaska, I never got the chance to ask.

A few years later and he was home visiting, tying up loose ends after his dad shot himself, when he met my mom in the Elks Club where she was bartending. Dad was half famous at home by then. He brought back bear teeth and coolers full of fish and stories that nobody could sniff for bullshit. Soon he'd knocked up my mom and they took up residence at Laurel Lane.

The best part of growing up in a trailer park is the fact that everyone around you lives in a trailer park, too. But we all had something to make the other kids jealous. Nick Destin's dad splurged on Pepsi in cans and his mom came to pick him up in a Mustang. The Patels got to go to New York City every winter to see their family. And me? I had my dad's stories. He talked about commercial fishing like some guys talk about war. They'd crowd around the little fire ring outside, holding cases of beer like suitcases, tossing the empties in the grass for my mom to pick up in the morning. Sometimes they let me stand around. Sometimes when it got late Mom would open the door and scream at them to quiet down and they would bitch and moan and finally relent.

Then something happened with NAFTA and the EPA and there were no local jobs and my dad said he had to go find work in Alaska. First, just for the summer. Then, summer salmon, winter crabbing. His buddies started stopping by a lot. Just to check-in, just to say *Hey.* Just to wink and tell my mom her hair looked good.

"Shame," they'd say. "Must be hard on a boy to go this long without his dad around."

It was a few years of that. Back and forth. He mailed us money. He couldn't call as much as he'd like. Most of my memories of him are from the winter. He brought me fake mukluks and stuffed polar bears and one round pin made of whalebone scrimshawed with the image of guess what?

Blub.

(In my slime line daydreams, I keep that pin in my pocket through the whole season and then I pitch it off the dock at sunset. But really, I couldn't tell you what happened to it. Haven't seen it in years.)

The first dead animal I ever saw up close was a squirrel, killed by a hawk and left in the yard behind the trailer. I remember feeling so humiliated to see its guts. The shame of being a witness. Ribbons of intestines, that little twisted neck. (Can you believe that before I created my own immersion therapy program I used to be so fucking squeamish?) My mom lifted it by the tail and dropped it with this unforgettable wet thud into the trashcan.

Then there was a roadkill buck that dad brought home for what I now know was an insurance scam. It was hunting season, when all the deer were huddled up at the edge of town. Sometimes, at dinner, my mom would say *Hey Look* and the three of us, or just the two of us, would sit with our forks dangling and watch the deer at her bird feeder, standing on their back legs, gnawing at the suet.

I was playing outside when I noticed some spots like red M&M's in the snow by the truck bed. I climbed on the bumper and there was this deer with legs scrambled at sharp angles. I just stared. The huge dead coat-button eyes. One of them swollen, ready to pop. I remember holding the frozen rail of the tailgate and wanting to let go but I couldn't. I couldn't look, couldn't look away. Even when the puke came rising.

Hey Look.

That's how it feels sometimes now—like I'm seven again, balancing on the bumper of that fucking truck, but it's my dad in the truck bed. His head is dented. His eyeball's hanging by a tendon. It's fluttering at the end of the nerve. Is he trying to look back at me? Pritchard used to tell me to finish intrusive thoughts, let the scenario play out, but I never make it to the end. It just keeps looping. The feeling? Not even grief. More like horror—disgust and rage and fear and something else, stored way down below the place where I keep my words.

I was staring at that buck when dad said, "Fuck's wrong with you?" He was carrying some rope and a cinder block from the shed.

"Did you hit this deer?"

"Not yet."

A couple of days later the insurance agent came to check out dad's smashed truck and wrote him a check for the damages. I heard him telling mom that the transmission was slipping. He took another two trips back-and-forth, and then poof, smoke, fuck, just mom and me.

The Klak Fancy Letter
Friday, June 23rd

Hello Klakers,

Great work so far. Remember that the first 2 hours of work performed on every new job is considered training, which means you must clock out when you switch jobs. We will be changing jobs often as we adjust to the skills and interests of our workers!

Important News:

*You must be processing fish by the official start time of your shift! The start time isn't the time that you clock in! The start time is the *latest possible time* that you can begin working. Therefore, you must clock in at least <u>9 minutes</u> before your shift.

*Please don't feed the foxes that you see around the processor grounds. Foxes carry rabies!

*The company store is out of international phone cards but will have more in the next 10 days.

*Please be mindful about what you're flushing because the septic system is under a lot of pressure during this time of the year.

Fish Count: 90,465 (That's nothing!)

Weather: High of 64, light rain. Sunrise—5:17 a.m. Sunset—11:40 p.m.

Alaska Word of the Day: Civil Twilight—The term for dusk or dawn, when the sun has sunk below the horizon but there's still enough light to see. If you factor in the long periods of civil twilight around sunrise and sunset, we have almost 24 hours of light this time of year.

Seven

Moonwalking. I could feel my feet going backward. Back to herring, back to this one weird thing I did at college, something I'll never share, and past it. To that phone call from my mom—Splat. Past that—Laurel Lane. I feel like a scared kid again. Just a little fucking duckling. A fuckling. Sour questions, burning on the way back up. Three days blowing chunks all over the boatyard—

Did you know a Duane Deaver?

Did you know a Joe Deaver?

Duane from Pennsylvania?

Little town called Bradford, Pennsylvania?

No one knew. Nobody had time. Don't you know the fish are starting? I was all knotted up, breaking down, freaking out, melting inside, until, Thank God, the season came to save me. Because when there's fish, everything here's beautiful. The processor's beautiful like an athlete or a machine or a highway interchange. It's honed violence. Compared with herring, salmon are huge and shiny and smell like clean salt. Yesterday, walking through fish house, I watched the first fat sockeye tick along the conveyor toward the header and gutter and felt embarrassed that I'd ever been excited about the piddlepiss herring we'd processed in spring. Salmon are the fucking money shot. I see why he liked them so much.

At high tide the tender takes the river and docks below the boatyard. The salmon are sucked uphill to the cannery with a hose the diameter of a basketball, landing in a huge concrete pool, fenced from bears. Most of the fish are dead but some of them still flop around the bloody water, searching for a spot to dump their genetic material. Milt, by the way, is just a fancy word for jizz.

Another tube draws the fish from the tank into the plant where they land on a long conveyor that guides them to the header and gutter. The header and gutter, which heads and guts, is a hoop as tall as a person and looks like the ring of fire from the county fair. A worker loads a fish into the hoop and presses a button and the fish is spun along the hoop on a track. Little blades slit the belly and the centrifugal force sucks out its guts. The fish goes around the hoop and stops, where its head gets lopped off by a blade that drops down like a guillotine and a worker tugs out any straggling guts. Each fish takes three seconds to head and gut. Sometimes the fish are still alive on the way to the h&g and it's someone's job to handle it. I watched the Turkish dude who does this job. He grabs two fish by the tails and slaps them together like he's uncaking mud from new school shoes. If a fish goes through the h&g conscious, it flails in the machine, gets tossed from the track half-spun, inside-out, and flops on the floor until someone gives it a stomp. That part of the plant's called fish house.

From fish house, the headed and gutted salmon take a short ride on a conveyor to the carnitech. What happens inside the carnitech, I don't know. It's just a big shining machine. It looks like it should make a car part, not fish fillets. An h&g salmon goes into one side and two long fillets pop out the other and fall onto opposite sides of a slime line—a long conveyor where foreign kids stand in one place, hunched over the belt, sixteen hours a day, trimming belly fat from fillets with electric knives that send scales and fat flying in every direction. Slime lining is the easiest/worst job at the cannery. It's mindless, mindless and purgatorial.

I'm over near the slime line on my break, watching the carnitech spit fillets, thinking how weird it is that nobody's ever stuck their hand inside, when Ernesto, the slime line foreman, yells for that Turkish kid Bayram in the you-fucked-up kind of voice. I turn and standing next to Ernesto, there's a cop in his full blues. Gun belt and everything. He's got red hair and razor burn like chicken skin and before I can look busy, he says, "You. In the freezer suit."

That's me. I like to keep my suit on, even on break. I like for people to know what I do.

"Come here a minute."

Ernesto's a full head shorter than the cop, built like a tea pot, and he's giving me a squirrely look, tilting his round head. It's the kind of look a person has when an elevator deposits them on a floor they've never seen.

"Couldn't help but notice your face," the cop says. The gash on my forehead's bandaged with a square of gauze. "Looks like maybe you got hit with a club or something."

Now Bayram's standing right next to me, eyes forward. All three of them are waiting, and one bad knife on the slime line behind us is squealing like murder, and that chicken skin under the cop's chin makes me want to vomit. I slipped on the ice in the blast freezer. Whacked my head on a pallet jack. First day of the season. The first hour, in fact. The first hour or the last, half asleep or dead tired, that's when the accidents happen, you know?

"A pallet jack," he says. "You hit your head on a pallet jack."

"I hit my head on a pallet jack."

"You smirking at me?" he says. "I thought your friend here was the funny one."

"That's just his face," Ernesto says. "He's always got that stupid grin."

"That's what happened, Ernesto? Pallet jack."

"I didn't see it," Ernesto tells him. "Might be an injury report somewhere if you want to take a look."

"Not right now," the cop says. His face is going pink in the cold. "Just keep this one on the processor grounds, huh?"

He turns to Bayram, looks him over, curls his lip. Everything about him looks like a cop, like my mom's husband. He says, "And this here's the comedian."

"Sir?"

"Oh cut the shit," he says, pulling a slip of paper from his pocket. "I don't know where in fuck's sake you're from. But here, police got actual work to do. You think I have time to handle some dumb pranks about human remains?"

He's holding my note. I start to tell him, I can feel the explanation push its way to the inside of my teeth, then it hits me that he'd know I was in Klak that night. It'd be so easy to drag me down to Klak so the bartender could point me out.

He says, "You think you're clever. Not clever enough to cross your whole name from the back of this."

"I have never been to Klak," Bayram says. "I swear it."

"He swears it," Ernesto says.

"He swears it," I say.

Bayram looks so scared, frozen with fear. Big, wild eyes like a trashcan raccoon. I feel awful. I never even bothered to look on the back of that scrap of paper. The cop waves it in his face.

"I got my eye on you," he says. "I got my eye on both of you."

"One eye," I say to him. "One eye for the both of us?"

"Both eyes, you shit." The cop takes a few steps away, stops. "One eye for each of you."

Ernesto cuffs me on the back of the head and follows the cop out, trying not to laugh, leaving Bayram and me standing on the slime line floor. There's four carnitechs, and four slime lines after them, a hundred newbie workers in their matching yellow raingear, all speckled with scales, all staring at us, hiss-whispering over the din of the knives. Fillets flying past them untrimmed and hitting the steel catch at the end of the conveyor, right by where we're standing. One every couple of seconds.

Fillet.

After fillet.

After fillet.

I might've fucked up real good with that bone and that bar and that photo.

Fillet.

Fillet.

Fillet.

Dozens piling up at the end of the slime line like they're looking for their lost other halves. They're spilling onto the heavy rubber anti-slip mats on the floor now—the kind we hose down after every shift but never get clean—and the slime line foremen are yelling for the workers to pick up those missed fish. It's like tossing ten-dollar bills on the floor, one foremen says.

"I don't understand what just happened," Bayram says.

"Me neither."

The foreman's yelling every motherfucker back to work when a forklift carrying a tub of chilled h&gs comes screaming through the heavy plastic strip curtains that separate the fish house from the slime line. The driver's hollering MOVE, and I pull Bayram out of the way. For a second the smell of propane overtakes us, then the fish stink comes roaring back.

"My sister told me this would happen," Bayram says. "She said, 'You go over there and you will be treated poorly, confused for Arab.' I said it was fine. I said I was the man of the house, and I had a plan."

Now Ernesto's marching back toward us and there's no hope in Bayram's face so I start spitting bullshit about how nothing bad can happen to him because I got his back and because I'm kind of the man of the house over in the packing department. Mr. Pritchard used to tell me that confidence is contagious, and yeah, I say, Bayram, I'm pretty important.

Then Helen is sticking a megaphone through the strip curtain that separates the slime line from packing and announcing to the whole world that if I'm not back in the freezer in one minute she's going to rip off my teeny tiny little balls.

"Yes," he says. "Very important."

"We'll talk about this later, motherfuckers," Ernesto says, smacking me on the forehead with his glove as he passes. Now there's slime on my bandage.

"One second," I yell to Helen.

"Now," she says. "I feel like a one-legged man in an asskicking contest over here."

She says that all the time.

I tell Bayram I'll get to the bottom of whatever that cop was talking about.

Eight

My old guidance counselor Mr. Richard Pritchard knew a learning disability when he saw one. He spared me the *follow your dreams* bullshit, which I appreciate, because I never had any to begin with. He always told me that finding a decent job is a process of elimination. I remember thinking of that during my first week at the processor, back in late March, standing there on the slime line, just like Bayram, the same socked-in-the-gut look, the same realization that I was all alone for a sixteener with my brain and all it could do. That was herring season and I remember the flesh flaking off them in the exact color and shape of teeth. Whose teeth? What balcony? What now? Four days of that, just me and the slime line din, when Helen found me in the breakroom with a freezer suit over her shoulder. She held it up to me, checked the fit.

She said, "You look like you're in great shape."

I said I do two-hundred pushups a day.

She said, "You're not dyslexic, are you? You gotta log numbers."

I said I had a BA in accounting.

She said, "Would you consider yourself a self-starter?"

I said, "There's literally not a single thing wrong with me," and started stripping off my raingear. "Should I just throw these out?"

After my first few hours in the freezers I was pulling fish racks faster than they were getting loaded, beating the slime line. I watched the freezers empty and refill and when my first shift ended, the only thing I could imagine wanting was my bed. I'd never felt that way before—not even a feeling, but a sub-feeling, like a compass or the limbo before a good sneeze. I told myself I'd chase that feeling down or die trying. I feel bad for Bayram, I do, but my hands are full. I'm squeezing my future by the throat. I'm the only one that can stop me. That shit at the bar was Exhibit A. Pritchard called it *impulsive behavior.* My mom just called it whimsy. Those lizard-brained things from way down at the base of the skull? That's my problem. That's how I got here. More or less.

One time, walking home from high school, I saw this guy pumping gas into a slick white Mercedes at the Sheetz. He had sunglasses on his head and few gray tufts of hair at his temples, like feathers. He was wearing cargo shorts with no signs of cargo. Our eyes locked and he grinned and this urge came over me. Not an urge, more like a need, a bodily function—I just had to fuck with him.

I said, "Wow, sick Cadillac!"

He laughed and shook the tip of the fuel nozzle three times before putting it back into the pump. "It's a Mercedes."

I asked if he was sure and he said he was.

"Have you checked the user's manual?"

He bent down and pointed at the chrome Mercedes logo.

"Cadillac makes Mercedes, I think," I said.

He said, "Funny guy." He wasn't annoyed and I hated him for it.

I said, "I read car magazines, okay?" and opened my eyes as wide as I could. So wide I could hardly see. So wide my eyeballs itched at the hidden spaces that rarely touched air. I saw it in him. His pity. How was I so dumb, could I even read, could my family not afford glasses, did my parents have jobs, were they cousins, was I in fact slobbering, how can someone be this fucking dense?

I said, "Let's just see if it's real!"

Then I was bending over the hood ornament chewing lightly.

I said, "I think it's a hard cheese!"

When he pushed me, and it wasn't even much of a push, I flopped on the pavement and wailed ASSAULTING A MINOR. He peeled tire out of there, hacked a curb on the way out.

But that's not how I got here.

That's just some context—

Generic State, a few days after my dad died, and I was knocking on an apartment door looking for this guy who sold me Adderall. At the apartment threshold, a fake-tanned white girl with a feather in her hair. Her name was Kristin, or maybe Kirstin, and this wasn't the right apartment. But she was playing a drinking game with four friends and would I like to join them?

Inside, a Derek. He was a criminology major, like me. I
remember a hookah on the coffee table and a mandala on the
wall and a tangle of video game bullshit on the floor. I was living
in a block dorm room with a future dental hygienist named
Mike, across the hall from two other guys named Mike. They
thought it was hilarious to tape down the button on cans of
AXE body spray and lob them into my room if I left the door
cracked.

Red Solo cups on the table and the slick of beer made it so
the cups drifted around for no reason, like they were being
manipulated by a frat boy's ghost. I'd been thinking a lot about
ghosts for the last few days.

While Kristin/Kirstin fills the cups, I ask Derek how he
liked CRIM 250.

"How'd you know I was in there?"

I said, "You sit in front of me. Glad to see your dandruff
has cleared up."

"That's weird, man," he said. "How do I not know you?"

"My name's Garrett Deaver."

(I wasn't an industrious motherfucker just yet.)

We stood in lines on each side of the table and chugged the
beer and flipped the cups and eventually I started to unfurl. I
started to think—no, know—that the insides of me were going
to come out. Like maybe my nerves would poke through my
pores and I'd be stuck that way forever, dragging around this
pain. Closing my nerves in car doors. Kids and stray dogs yank-
ing on my nerves. Everyone pointing, whispering about what

it must feel like. I could feel them, then, on the edge of breaking through. Sprouting. There was just too much pressure building up. Something had to give. I'd told nobody that my dad had died. At that point, I'd still thought it was an accident. That's what my mom had told me. That he fell, not jumped.

Derek from CRIM 250 said, "Yo, Barrett, let's play some more beer pong."

We did. He had no idea I was completely losing my shit. Every time he hit a cup, Derek flexed in a kidding/not kidding way. He kept saying shit like Drink Bitch and Who's Your Daddy. I thought it was my chance to say it out loud. Balcony. But Derek hit another cup before I could say anything and all at once I remembered that guy and his fucking Mercedes, and I looked down the pipeline of Derek's life and I saw the Mercedes that would be waiting for him, and I saw nothing waiting for me but sidewalk, and I was really losing my shit, and I thought, losing my shit—well, Fuck! I asked where the bathroom was and without thinking about it, with a distinct not-thinking-about-it, I went in there and closed the door and stopped to look at the white bath bomb on the tub rail that looked like a dislodged eye. I took the ceramic top off the toilet tank and set it on the lavender bathmat. I stood on the closed seat and leaned back until I found the spot where my energy could flow and my body did what my body needed to do. I put the lid back on, wiped my shoeprints, and went back to the party.

"Gotta run," I said. "Late for work."

"Work?"

"Yes, work! I'm a valet."

I stopped going to CRIM and a few days later my room-mate sent me a text asking if I'd shit in someone's toilet tank. He saw a post about it on Facebook. Everyone saw it on Facebook—some dude named Barrett from CRIM 250, a weirdo who parks cars drunk. It couldn't be me. That's what I told him and the Mikes across from us, and the Melissas down the hall and the Laurens past them. I'm Garrett, with a *G*.

On the way back from the dining hall, my pockets bulging with stolen Pop-Tarts, I turned the corner on my floor and saw that dude Derek pounding on my door. I left all my clothes in the closet and limped my old Kia back to my home-town, to Flex's house, where my mom had just moved in.

"I knew it," she said.

"You knew it."

"I knew you'd let this be an excuse."

The Klak Fancy Letter
Sunday, June 25th

Hello Klakers,

Are you sore yet? The first week or two is always the hardest! Especially with so many of us traveling from all over the world, it's natural for some germs to pass around. I want to urge everyone to wash their hands. We can offer you over-the-counter medications if necessary, but you need to just **tough it out.**

Important News:

*We're excited to welcome Nigel, Quality Control Expert from Thornrose Market, the UK's premier luxury grocery chain. Klak Fancy is honored to be the first exclusive salmon provider for Thornrose Market.

*Cigarettes can be purchased at the company store, open every break. Everything you want can be deducted from your paycheck.

*We've been dismayed to hear rumors of some of our workers' behavior in Klak. There is **no need** to go to Klak. We **will** lock down the processor grounds if necessary.

*Laundry service is suspended for the next 3 days.

Fish Count: 147,000 (We have a long way to go to make FISH 101 for each shift!!!)

Weather: High of 67 (very warm!), clear. Sunrise—5:18 a.m. Sunset—11:40 p.m.

Alaska Word of the Day: The Bush—Alaskans refer to areas of the state that aren't accessible on the road system as "the bush." Alaska is nearly three times as big as the next biggest American state (Texas) and the vast majority of Alaska is the bush.

Nine

The alarm clocks writhe like a mass poisoning. One, then two, then the whole line of them down the bunkhouse start seizing. Hands pop up and smack them quiet again. But there's always one left ringing, or knocked on the floor, or thrown against a wall, and at the other end of the bunkhouse some sleeping kid sits up and yells. The language doesn't matter—*shut the fuck up* is all context. It's easy to turn over, hide your head with a pillow. Go back to whatever you were dreaming. Was that even him in the picture? Does it even matter? All the creaking cots, the scattered blankets. Farts and cracked knuckles. The kinds of stuff that used to make me sick, back before I swallowed it. Every day I make a point to spring out of my cot. I make a point to say Good Morning. I manifest the man I want to be. Look: I don't have to do this. I *get* to fucking do this—long underwear and inner socks and neoprene socks and jeans and boots and thermal and orange beanie. First out the door, motherfuckers, clicking my heels to the chow house.

Peoples' hands hurt. Their feet. Their necks are so stiff they can hardly look up. But nobody said this would be all tits and honey. They stand around with their sore hands on hot coffee. They tip forward, snap awake. The line between days feels made up, like a border. Every day somebody says Fuck, it feels like I *just* went to sleep.

I say, Flash-freezing preserves freshness, and nobody ever laughs.

Get gloves, liners, hair and beard nets. The iodine boot dip health code bullshit. I check the fish counts. Shift A got the bonus. Shift B is a bunch of pussies. I slip into my freezer suit, button the legs, zip myself up to the neck. Some days I wish I knew a prayer. Something to keep me focused. A sixteener can take on the feeling of a whole life if you let it. On my bad days, and I've had too many since seeing that photo, I start off confused like a baby. Then I daydream like a kid, thinking of all things I could be. Eight hours in and reality hits. This is my job, my future, I got to make the most of it. That's when I peak, baby—I actualize, I'm the man of the house now. I see everything, I'm everywhere, there's more than one of me, and if I could look down from the catwalk and see myself, I'd see a whole family of me, clones filling out logbooks while pulling racks while chipping ice while sorting fillets while loading freezers while filling out logbooks while pulling racks, while, while, while—

After maybe thirteen hours I start to stoop. I can feel my own hair turn gray. By quitting time, I'm shitting myself, sundowning, forgetting my own name, looking for my dead dad, crying for him at bedtime. That's why you got to hone it in. Just think *Blub*. The accelerol helps, when I can get it. Kiddie speed—caffeine wrapped in codeine wrapped in B-12. That shit is golden. It makes your heart into a hummingbird. Illegal in forty-seven states.

God Bless the great states of Mississippi, North Dakota, and Alaska.

Get to work.

What else helps get me through the day? Making lists of everything I love about the freezers—

1. Physically, it's hard as fuck. You got these three-hundred-pound racks of freezing trays coming off the slime line, maybe two racks a minute full-up with wet fillets, a couple hundred per rack, and you got to run—sometimes, literally, run—over to the slime line and push the racks into packing, and the wheels on the racks are always going squirrely, and the strip curtain's always catching on your rack, and the freezer door latch is stuck, and Helen's screaming, and the blood and slime's frozen so thick on the freezer wall that you have to chip it with the ice hammer to make the racks fit, and then there's something in your eye, a scale maybe, a scratch, who knows, no time, blink it away—more racks.

2. Mentally, you got to always be thinking, killing the unwanted and/or intrusive thoughts. Like the other day, I remembered how after my dad left, my mom would throw out his mail immediately so I only ever saw his name in the trash, but before I could get too deep into it, I had to fill out a logbook about which fish went

to which freezer and when, or else the British QC guy would be all over my ass, asking questions.

3. When it's time to empty a freezer, you open the door and the cold oozes across the concrete floor like it was conjured by a wizard and the packing department workers start to shiver in their rain gear and goddamn, I like the power in that.

4. In addition to the six regular freezers there's a blast tunnel—a fifty-foot tube, -35 degrees, swirling wind, freezes PREMIUM fillets in ten minutes—and if you spit in the empty blast tunnel, your spit spirals and freezes and explodes at the other end. Or at least I think so. I've looked at the other end and found nothing, and if there's nothing where there was something, explosion is always a possibility, right?

5. Freezer guys are important and finding good ones is tough and so apparently you can cause a scene at a bar in Klak and everything will be chill.

6. To learn the freezers is to learn the processor—the rhythms, the flow, the pinch points and trouble spots. Helen was a freezer worker before her promotion, and she's told me on two distinct days that freezer workers are usually tapped for supervisor jobs and when she said it, I knew that she was speaking *rhetorically*, because I took that shit in college, and even though I don't agree that everything we say/do is rhetorical, in this instance, it was.

SLIME LINE / 67

7. Accelerol!

8. $2.50 more per hour than the slime line or the packing floor, and I got debt coming out my ass.

9. There's a metal catwalk that runs above the freezers, above the partition walls that separate fish house from the slime line from packing, and sometimes Kevin Haverberger likes to pace the catwalk and watch us work. Sometimes I look up and he's looking at me and he nods and I nod back to him. I hope he can hear me talking to his processor, even if he doesn't know it speaks back—

Shhhhhh.
Each fillet's a red, wet tongue.
They're saying, "Garrett, processor prince. Welcome to your future."

Ten

I'm standing at the lip of the loading dock thawing the frozen legs of my suit for a minute, just enough so the knees will bend again. It's windy, low clouds bullying their way in from the bay. An eagle flies by with a vacuum pack in its claws, over the cannery grounds in a second, shooting upriver—gone. People always want to be birds, but me?

Blub.

On the gravel below the dock, where we load the shipping containers, a yellow dog all lumpy with tumors stops to piss on the tire of a shitty pickup. Then the dog jumps. Another rock sails past and cracks the door of the truck and now the dog's hobbling away. I look around the corner and the old drunk from the bar is standing there with a handful of stones.

Joe. I heard he fell off something and died.

I'm in the air by the time I think, Mistake! Delete! My job! Racks of fish on the floor and a freezer door half open! But I'm already in the gravel out front of the loading dock and the sky's suddenly silver and the wind smells like answers and a truck driver's shrieking his airhorn at me because he's got to back up another shipping container into the bay. I wave him on, fake an *official business* walk around the side of the building, and now I'm running. The old drunk's not in front of the chow house, where retired fishermen try to show up and sneak lunch. He's not in the break room bumming smokes from Turks and he's not at the front desk in the office telling bad jokes to the ladies who work there. He's not in the shower house—I even kicked open one shitter stall door like a cop and all I saw was a Colombian kid asleep on the toilet—and he's not anywhere. Add this to my long list of mistakes because I keep running laps around the grounds, and each step I take is like a clock ticking and each tick of the clock is a fish going bad on the floor.

Past the shower house and the chow house and the truck again and this must be what they mean when they talk about magnetite—the need to know like a compass, like a drug, like a door slamming shut, locking me from my work. Those fish are going soft. Maybe I can use the bathroom excuse? Diarrhea works if you don't overuse it. Or I ran a rack over my foot. Something, anything. Who the fuck is Joe?

I see him then, just a glimpse, way down past the bunkhouse, by Bonnie's shack.

Go—

The thinking comes when the running stops, at the edge of the dunes, crouched at the back of Bonnie's shack. It hits me that he might think I'm a criminal. He might've gotten in some trouble for shooting a gun in a bar. That cop has already got at least one eye trained on me. And how close was this old fuck, really, to leveling that gun at me? He could have killed me! And now we're going to chat? What a little fuckling. So like a duckling, I get low. I waddle and crawl around the side of the shack, sand worming into my freezer suit, and when I peek around the other side, I can see that he's talking to Bonnie. I can't see her but his hands are up, like he's the one with a barrel pointed at him. I know that posture. I've been doing it my whole life. *Let me explain.* What is he explaining? There's noise in the boatyard and the wind's starting to rattle the riggings but beneath it I hear Bonnie's voice say my name.

What about me?

A curtain of rain moving up from the bay.

I listen, nothing, the curtain drops.

Hard, cold, sideways rain and I crawl back through the wet sand and shake it from the legs of my freezer suit and I got a mobius strip of problems by the time I get back to the processor. I can't get back through the main doors without clocking in, and I can't clock in because I didn't clock out. I circle the building, settle on the loading dock, climb up on the bumper of a docked truck, and squeeze between the shipping container and the bay door. Someone closed my freezers and the newbies are pulling the racks on the floor to their lines. If this were mid-season, we'd be deeply fucked. But now it looks survivable. The catwalk's empty and Helen isn't around either.

It's possible nobody even noticed.

It's possible this all might work—

"You missed the Iodine dip for your boots."

The QC inspector is staring at me in his stupid white coat. He's wearing a beard net even though he's clean shaven. Says everything you need to know about him.

He says, "Your logs say those fish were on the floor for fourteen minutes. They can't sit for more than ten with downgrading from Excellent to Great."

I say, "Let me explain."

". . . And where's your beard net?"

". . . And why are you so sandy?"

". . . And so goddamned wet?"

". . . And my god, that wound on your head is leaking! David Beckham buys this salmon and you're handling it with a bleeding head!"

Before I can speak, he's scribbling notes on his clipboard and I'm down on my dirty knees praying to the QC gods for forgiveness.

Eleven

After I left the upper-decker and split Generic State, I had no place to go. Alaska wasn't even the plan. There was no plan. I just laid on the pullout in Flex's basement for three days watching war footage on the old TV he used mostly for porno. My mom wouldn't even look at me, so I wasn't surprised when I heard the heavy sound of Flex's boots coming down the steps. We barely knew each other, but he paid me to cut his firewood the few times I came to visit from college. He liked to fold up the money, hand it to me, and pull it away when I reached for it. I had to say thanks first.

So there's Flex. He and my mom got together about two years earlier, right around the time I started putting my tuition on the credit card. My mom had hit me with this philosophy about turning twenty: how the year twenty meant success and balance because it was ten *plus* ten—the merger of the spiritual and material something-something. She said I wouldn't *actually* turn twenty unless I embraced what it meant to turn twenty. You see? I wouldn't want to be nineteen forever. Success meant independence. Independence meant I was cut off from any financial help, not that she had much anyway. I never should have been in college in the first place. But I didn't know that then, and nobody other than Mr. Pritchard had the balls to say the quiet part out loud.

In the basement, Flex sat down next to me. "If I was any younger," he said, "that's where I'd be." Tracer rounds were zipping across the TV screen. You could see a city skyline in the second after something exploded. Quick as a blink. I knew what he was getting at. I thought it'd be pretty sad for me to blow up the first real city I ever visited.

He said, "You gotta leave the nest!" and slapped my knee. "I vowed to stay out of it, but now you're tiptoeing around my house in the dark. I'm a cop. I got sensitive ears."

I said, "Makes sense. Your ears are fucking huge."

He slapped my knee again and held his hand there for a second too long. He liked that, knowing he could. He suggested the air force and that's when the word came, just like the upper-decker. It flowed. I wasn't even sure what I had said until he repeated it.

"Alaska? You gotta be fucking kidding me."

"I already got a job lined up."

"What a vindictive little bitch you are," he said.

That night, I walked around downtown Bradford, all three blocks of it. In an apartment above the closed Chinese restaurant two tweakers were arguing about a missing lighter. It scared the shit out of me, like my future was already written on one of those dank apartment walls, and I thought maybe Flex was right about the air force. Then I ran into Nick Destin, my old buddy from Laurel Lane, on his way into the American Legion. He had a goatee like he'd written the letter O in fur around his lips. He told me he and his girlfriend had twins and their names were Hunter and Trapper. He said he worked as a 911 dispatcher.

I said, "You must really hear some bad shit."

He said, "After a while, it's only bad when you know the people."

If Nick knew my dad had died, he didn't mention it. He did say he saw my mom in the Market Basket and heard I was doing great and graduating soon.

"Just did," I said. "Logistics. But I got a job in Alaska. Computer stuff. Freight."

I was halfway back to Flex's before I started thinking about what Nick said. Did my mom talk to him before she knew I'd quit school, or was she too ashamed to tell the truth? Half the dudes in my hometown quit college. They ended up working at the particleboard plant. The guys who never bothered leaving home were their supervisors.

In the basement I applied to every job I could find. I was still at it when Flex came down the next morning and said we needed to get serious. I told him I was as serious as his haircut. You could set a plate on the top of it.

"Look," he said. The ceiling was low, just rafters, and he liked to hang from them when he talked to me so I could see how strong he was.

He said, "Would it change your mind if I told you your father killed himself?"

"Fuck you."

"Makes sense," he said. "Think about it."

He looked serious to me then. He looked like a cop. He even used a deep cop voice when he explained. First, they got a call from some guy in Alaska who knew my dad. That guy just said he died, fell off a balcony in Hawaii. That's the news my mom gave me. A few days later she got another call, this time from a coroner. He said something about the way my dad's legs were broke. There's a certain way with suicides. *Burst fractures*—the femurs explode.

I said to Flex, "What exactly did the coroner say? Is there a report or something?"

He said there wasn't.

I asked if he had the number for that guy in Alaska.

He said he didn't have it, and I said bullshit.

"This is why your mom didn't want to tell you," he said. "Figured it'd send you off your rocker again."

I told him it didn't matter. Good jobs in Alaska, I said.

He handed me a check for a thousand bucks. I tore it up, said I was good on money, put the plane ticket on that credit card, cut up the card, and peace'd.

Twelve

It's past lunch when Helen tracks me down. I fucked up, I know, I earned whatever bag of shit she'll give me. My guess is she'll make me clean toilets. I saw it happen during herring season, when some kid got busted sneaking down to the chow house mid-shift to barter cigarettes for ice cream. He told me why he did it too. Every night, he said, he'd been dreaming that we processed ice cream instead of herring. Cartons of it coming down the line. When he tried that explanation on Helen, she didn't even crack a smile. He had to stay at the end of every sixteener and scrub the scales and piss stains off the bathroom walls.

I'll take it as a test of my stomach.

I'll take it with a smile.

She's whistling for me from the top of the catwalk and I jog across the packing floor, hoping she's watching, and I punch the strip curtain out of my way and climb the clanging metal stairs up to the top, where I can see the whole plant like a pale blue dot. None of it looks chaotic from up top. The forklifts hauling huge blue tubs of chilled fish look synchronized, taking turns through the strip curtain to the carnitech. Even the slime line looks perfect and clean. All the slime liners, shoulder-to-shoulder, headless in their yellow hoods, like one long centipede, a hundred arms reaching out from one yellow body. At the end of the line that Bayram kid is sweeping scraps into the open grate that leads to the chummer. It's perfect, the processor, and it hits me how lucky I am to be here and how I've never been good at anything else, and how I almost let my dad take it from me, and I'm ready to scrub anything.

We're clopping toward each other and I watch her face grow and sharpen into focus and think that maybe I'll explain about my dad and the picture but now her lips are starting to move and I can't hear what she is saying because of the freezer noise and because I'm distracted by the railing, wondering whether its higher or lower than my dad's, and who the fuck commits suicide on vacation, in paradise, and all I catch from Helen is *slime line*. I just stare. Crust in the corner of one eye. Blood vessels like photographed lightning. She's saying she didn't expect this reaction and I remember to flatten my smile.

"Is this because of the bartender?"

"What bartender?" She's shaking her head and pointing toward Kevin's office. Her head is floating, just bobbing in the air, disconnected. She says, "Kevin just left me a note. Said you missed the boot dip."

"You're fucking joking. Everyone misses the boot dip."

"And the racks you left on the floor?"

"Dock my pay," I say. "Cut the whole day from my timecard." She's shaking her head and where did her body go—

"And I'll do the bathrooms."

Nothing.

"Before and after every shift."

She says, "Garrett, last week we had a cop asking about you on the slime line floor. Today, the Brit from QC was up here threatening to downgrade a week's worth of fish. What the fuck else do you expect me to do?"

"This isn't me," I tell her. "I just have some family stuff—"

"I don't care," she says, "There's extra raingear in the rubber room. Write your name on it."

Behind the processor is the break room and annexed to that is the rubber room, where rows of yellow raingear hang. If your eyes are wet and your vision's blurry with rage, the rubber room looks like a slaughterhouse for Big Bird's family. I punch the first bib I see, wishing there was meat inside of it. I take my time with the freezer suit, sniffing hard at the dizzy bleach smell. If I can just talk to Kevin. I'd say it was just a couple of racks. Just a little iodine. The freezers are important. I am important! This is *my* job. Or it is my *job*. *My* job, my *job*—by the time I sit down in the break room, something like mold is creeping into the corners of my eyes. A little white streak at the edge of things. And now I'm imagining myself filling with sand, Pritchard's old trick, slow and heavy and cool, until the breath catches. Heavy like an X-ray blanket—slow, heavy, slow, slower, Garrett, and soft, and slow, and heavy, and cool, Garrett, and soft, and heavy, and cool, and slower, and when I'm full of sand, there's no space for anything else.

But it won't work now and in the corner of the rubber room there's this bucket of bleach and I stick my head into it and whiff and whiff and whiff and whiff and gasp and whiff until the room rotates and after I get up off the floor, I try to rub that thing out of my eye and can't.

Fuck it. I grab some new raingear and write my name on the jacket before even unfolding it. When I put it on, it says—

The Klak Fancy Letter
Thursday, June 29th

Hello Klakers,

I'm seeing some sore young men and women limping around the processor. Get all of the sleep that you can, and keep your eyes on the prize. It's a long season and your body will adjust. If this was easy, anyone could do it.

Important News:

*Our cleaners have noticed a lot of boot prints on the toilet seats. Please do not stand on the toilet seats!!! Take a seat. You've earned it.

*It seems like some workers have been abusing the hot water in the processor bathroom. Please only use as much as you need to maintain cleanliness.

*Cigarettes can be purchased at the processor store, open during every break.

*Laundry service has resumed.

Fish Count: 277,843 (Big improvement, folks.)

Weather: High of 63, rain. Sunrise—5:20 a.m. Sunset—11:39 p.m.

Alaska Word of the Day: Fishery—Fishery is the practice of harvesting fish from a specific region, and also the name applied to specific habitats where fish are harvested. The Bristol Bay sockeye salmon fishery is managed by the Alaska Department of Fish and Game.

When the Bristol Bay sockeye fishery was decimated by overharvesting in the early 1900s, processing facilities pooled their money and funded some of the first large-scale fisheries research on Earth. Today, Bristol Bay remains the gold standard for sustainable management worldwide.

Thirteen

You catch a fillet coming off the carnitech, turn it belly down, trim the white fat from the meat with an electric knife. That's it. That's all you do. That's the job. My job. Me. You wear a chain-mail glove on one hand, so you couldn't cut yourself even if you tried. I tried, got my glove stuck, broke my knife, got a bag of shit from Ernesto.

Welcome to hell.

Turns out that hell's not hot. It's not cold either. It's probably the temperature you feel at the exact moment you die. A non-feeling. A non-temperature. Mr. Pritchard told me that's why people slit their wrists in the bathtub, because the water's the same temp as your blood. He said life leaves easier if it's draining into familiar territory. He said those people wanted death without the dying. That motherfucker said this to me in the tenth grade, after I told him that my grandpa and his brother had both committed suicide. What would he say if I called that my magnetite? We met once a week for six years, and I still don't even know. One week, he'd theme our session something like "The Clear Light of Reality" and paraphrase shit from *The Tibetan Book of the Dead*—"Death holds the all-seeing mirror of past actions," or "a useful faith should not be blind." The next week, we'd talk about trade school. One time he made a PowerPoint called Philosophy Buffett, where he shared life lessons from the Buffetts, Warren and Jimmy. I thought they were brothers.

Death holds an all-seeing mirror? If that was the case, I wouldn't have been chasing answers instead of loading fish racks. If that was the case, I wouldn't see my dad dead in the truck bed every time I try to blink that blurry spot from my eye. It's long and white and peripheral. Like a bone. Ha! What would've happened if people had walked past my dad on that sidewalk, saying he was just a bear? A bear's scrambled brains, a bear's pancaked face, a bear's bloody Aloha print shirt?

If no one had told me, he wouldn't be dead. There's your all-seeing mirror.

Fuck me, we're in the trouble now Beaver.

I've thought about killing myself plenty of times but never for any one reason. It's not even *sadness*. Not even a feeling, but something below a feeling. An impulse. That upper-decker. That jump from the loading dock. It just comes at me in these short videos that play behind my eyelids on the slime line. I'm hanging. I'm falling. I'm squeezing a trigger. There's no real reason. There's no real *why*. It's more passive—what if—than active. But there were a couple times in college when the active came screaming past the passive so fucking fast it scared the shit out of me. One time I caught myself tugging on the shower rod, and when it fell, I was so relieved I actually called up my mom to ask how she was doing. I didn't tell her anything because the worst of it was over. I didn't tell her anything because she'd be thinking *fate*—

Let's go get that fucking job back.

Fourteen

"It's you," Bonnie says, looking up. She's sitting at an upturned cable spool she uses like a table, scrubbing a rusty wok with steel wool. Christmas lights in the shack are twinkling, warm smoke at eye level, coffee smells. I'm standing in the doorway and I've got eight hours to talk and sleep and eat and shit before I get back to work. It's been two days on the slime line and now I got moves to make and I've been hoping Bonnie can help me make them.

"I was just thinking about you," she says. "Come out of that rain."

I can't be sure when anybody's ever said that to me before—*just thinking about you*—and I sit or maybe melt. Words mean more post-shift. Everything does. In the brake-check before you crash, you step out of the cannery and the whole world winks and says it's been going on without you. The eagles are meaningful. The ravens are meaningful. The pissing rain and the boat lights and the smoke from the fishing camps way across the river—

And Bonnie Kohle. Especially Bonnie Kohle, but I can't quite say why.

"It's never warm like this when it rains," she says. "It feels like California."

The wok she's scrubbing is the size of a hug and the rust leaves a halo on the table when I pick it up.

"I found it on the bunkhouse steps," she says. "Stolen from over there."

She points out the window, north of the processor, toward the alder brush and the creek past it. She's talking about the abandoned house in the woods past the shower house. Everyone calls it the bear house because one time when some cannery kids from Moldova went over there they supposedly saw a bear on the porch and came running back screaming BEAR HOUSE.

"This right there," she says, pointing at the wok, "that's why all the locals hate you little shits. Just take, take, take. It's the whole goddamned history of men in this state."

She looks tired, half-asleep still. A sunburn on her nose is starting to peel.

"Sixteener?"

I shake my head yeah.

"How's the slime line?"

"How'd you know that?"

"Jesus, Beaver," she says. "I know everything."

Then there's a coffee cup in my hand, a sour liquor smell rising with the coffee vapors. The mug's white and chipped and there's art on it, a small red bird in the belly of a blue bird, long black legs wrapped around the mug like they're trying to find my fingers and hold on.

"I made that," she says. "A long time ago."

I lay it out for her—how I just got behind on a couple of racks, something that happens all the time. How it was my first mistake on the job. How bad I need the job, the money, the future, the work, and what did she think?

"I think," she says. "I think you ought to toss a knife into the carnitech and run. The luddites were right."

I say I busted my ass for my job, and she says it's not *my* job. It's *a* job, and it exists with or without me, and the sooner I get that through my busted-up head, the better off I'll be. She gets like this sometimes. Contrarian. There'd be days working together preseason when I couldn't do a single thing right. Then the next day she'd praise me for the same thing.

"Look," she says. "And use your thinking brain."

She wiggles the fingers on her left hand. "This is you."

She wiggles the fingers on her right hand. "This is some other fucker."

She lifts her left hand up, and the right hand goes down, like a scale. "Wooop," she says. Again, in reverse. "This is how it works. Someone goes up, somebody else goes down."

I say, "I'm not an idiot. My point is about who deserves it."

"And that's you."

"That's me."

"And you're so sure?"

"I'm so sure."

She yanks the mug out of my hand and refills it for me from the pot on the stove. She says, "If you got this place all figured out, march up there and tell Kevin. Tell Ernesto, too.

Fuck, tell Helen and some of those foreign kids they stick on the line. Say you've been in Alaska for, what, almost three months and you deserve more from it. Tell them God put it here for Beaver Whatever your last name is."

There's a hardness in her face and when I try to speak I can feel my vocal cords warbling. She just keeps going.

She says, "While you're at it, walk into town and tell the first Native person you see that you deserve that spot in the freezer. Six thousand years of netting fish here, just waiting for you to show up."

I stand up, finish my mug. Waves of exhaustion pounding my legs. I tell her I'm sorry I came and interrupted her. I tell her I just wanted advice.

"I already told you. Sabotage."

I ask her if I did something to piss her off.

She just waves me away like I'm just smoke in her eyes.

"You're being really mean to me."

"God, listen to yourself. People are being mean to you! I'm the one that got you out of that trouble in the Black Dog. Paid off the bartender, talked down that old guy who came around looking for you. And you come down here whining to me because Kevin gave your job to his nephew?"

"Wait, what nephew?"

"Oh, fuck off, Garrett."

Fifteen

No sleep. Too much brutal snoring. Too much light knifing the gap in the blackout curtain. Blinding bright, deafening bright, and eyes closed ain't much better. They call it the slime line spins. Supposedly anybody who spends enough time staring down at a conveyor will get them. I can feel things moving in front of me. Inside of me. Even the darkness moves. Even when you're stuck you're moving. What's the lesson in that, Pritchard? I see the season passing. There goes my supervisor job. There goes Bonnie, and there goes my clarity, blown away by Bonnie. I hear her, I do, I'm a piece of shit. Not the first time, okay? Maybe I didn't deserve the freezer in the first place but stuck is stuck is stuck, and if I draw my pay and split Klak before the season ends, they'd take thirty bucks a day for room and board because it's in the contract, the one I helped the Turks sign, too, and stuck is stuck is stuck; they could subtract the ticket from Anchorage on top of room and board, and being stuck is barely having enough cash to get back home, and *stuck* is my herring pay going to some bills and *stuck* is my credit card in the trash back at Flex's place and *stuck* is the way Flex grabbed me by the arm before I left, and *stuck* is the way he said *don't come limping back* and *stuck* is the posture I took, shoulders back, fists twitching, and *stuck* is the promise. I told him I wouldn't. I told him he didn't know shit about me.

Sorry, Bonnie, but you don't know shit about me either.

But then again neither do I.

Other than the fact that I'm an industrious motherfucker.

What nephew? What fucking nephew?

Sixteen

In the morning the accelerol helps unstick me from my cot. What nephew? No new bodies in the bunkhouse, and I skip breakfast looking for answers. Ernesto will know what's up.

Ernesto's worked at Klak Fancy for like eight years. Before that he worked winters processing king crab out on the Aleutians and summers at an old-school cannery called Premium Red that was so sketchy they could barely find workers. People liked to say that at Premium Red Ernesto had been like a mob boss—keeping workers in line, taking handouts for promotions, selling illegal fish on the side. That place got shut down but Ernesto still liked to brag about it, even about the canning machine that took half of his middle finger. When somebody complains about being tired or sick, he shows them his finger and says, "This is how much I care." He's got a special status at the cannery, one that you get from saying yes to shit that other people say no to. He likes to steal a freezer suit and sleep off hangovers in the holding cooler. I caught him in there once, curled up like a cat on the top of a tote of fillets.

I catch him standing in a white patch of sun outside the break room, inhaling a bran muffin that looks like a baby's head. My accelerol's really starting to kick, I can feel it pulsing in my ears, and Ernesto's muffin is practically crying when he rips off a hunk. I tell him I need his help and I can tell that he likes it, being needed. There's a certain way he lifts his chin when I ask for his advice, a sureness that he has answers. Like Pritchard, like Flex, he knows he can alpha-dog me and I let him.

"Iodine's serious business," he says, sarcastically. He's eating and smoking at the same time, blowing yellow smoke from his nose while he chews.

"Was it about the cop?"

"One time," he says, "I got so drunk I crashed a Klak Fancy pickup into the gate outside Neptune." This is peak Ernesto right here. Only speaking in stories. "First thing, I called Kevin and told him I fucked up. He told me not to worry about it. He said everybody makes a little mistake. Then he sent somebody to pick me up. By noon the next day the gate was fixed and nothing else ever happened about it. No cops, nothing. So, no, Beaver, it's not about no fucking cop. Kevin's nephew needed a job. Between us he's a little bitch but it's not my problem."

I say, "You think it's right that some nephew gets to come eat my lunch?"

And just like Bonnie, Ernesto's got a hand in the air now. He's holding it sideways, showing me his cracked knuckles, the spotted brown skin. When you hold a hand that way, it takes the shape of Pennsylvania. It's how I explain to people where I grew up. I don't know if it's coincidence, but right near my hometown, in the North Central part, right near the New York border, a mangled middle finger rises up like a worm, wiggles, and disappears.

"Peek a boo," he says. "Welcome to the real fucking world."

I clock in and find a place on the slime line and when I look up, I'm rubbing shoulders with Bayram. "There he is," he says, slapping his rubber gloves together so the scales go flying. "There is a very important person."

"It's temporary," I say.

"There is the man of the house over in packing."

He looks at me like we're in on the same joke, and I guess we are. The most beautiful place on Earth, and all we get to see are these fillets three feet in front of us. It's not lost on me, the irony. I just got no time for irony.

Bayram and I are working across from a tiny Moldovan kid who has HARD WORKER written on the back of his jacket. He's super short with dark eyes and has a girlfriend who is super tall with scrunched shoulders, like she's trying to use them as earmuffs. They're always arguing over his hack job trimming. Whenever she wants to yell at him over all the noise, she has to bend way down to reach his ear. He scowls when men talk to her, but men always talk to her anyway, which makes his filleting worse, which makes them argue more, which makes men more interested in talking to her.

Bayram thinks it's hilarious. He tells me the first thing he learned in business school was never to mix business with pleasure. That was his first mistake here, he says, signing up his friends to come with him to Klak Fancy. His second mistake was somehow thinking everything would go as planned. He still hasn't figured out how he got wrapped up in this situation with the police.

"Do you know?" he says. "I still have no idea what he was talking about."

If only!

In the spring, I'd tried to make friends with four Moldovans in the bunkhouse who had this habit of sitting in a circle and whispering until they exploded laughing at something one of them said. If we made friends, I figured, I'd know they weren't laughing at me. One of them had a guitar and sang slow ballads in Romanian. When I asked him why the songs were so sad, he said I knew nothing about history.

I don't want to be so ignorant. I want to ask Bayram the right questions, but no matter what all I bring up, he just wants to talk shit on the processor. Hours, timecards, fish counters, overtime, bonuses—so many questions, and it hits me I don't have the answers.

"I don't know," I catch myself saying a lot. "I don't know, but I'll find out."

"That's okay," he says. "I'll take you over Jarrod Haverberger any day."

The nephew. Jarrod.

Bayram worked next to him for a few days. He said Jarrod claims to be training for a career as a cage fighter and walks around like it, always cracking his knuckles, always flexing, like he's carrying a tire under each arm. He called Bayram "kid" or "pal" and claimed Helen wanted to fuck him. He left the line to smoke whenever he felt like it, leaving fish piling up for the workers behind him.

"He's not in the bunkhouse," I say. "I haven't seen the fucker."

"He has his own shack."

Some of the second-year workers don't even have their own shacks!

"Go look into packing," he says. "Go fast and I will cover for you."

I cross the slime line floor and stick my head through the strip curtain into packing where the bay doors are open and there's light, real light, flooding in. There's a small bird stuck in packing and two Colombian workers are chasing it around, waving their yellow coats, laughing, yelling, trying to lead the bird back out the bay door. But it won't go. It keeps stopping to sit on the rafters and watch, and on the packing line everyone is distracted, and the bird swoops low, and two kids on the line duck, and even the QC guy is laughing, and then, pulling a rack from the blast tunnel, Jarrod appears. He's wearing my freezer suit, the one with the duct-taped knee. That's my tape. I put it there. It tore on the sharp corner of a rack a week ago, left my knee bloody. That suit was always a little too long in the legs for me. The bottoms would get wet and freeze solid. It fits him perfect. Bayram was right about the way he walks. Nobody's ever made him hurry. Nobody's ever told him how fucking stupid he looks.

I wonder how long it'd take him to freeze to death in the blast tunnel. Like, if something happened to the door, you know?

The Klak Fancy Letter
Monday, July 3rd

Hello Klakers,

Tomorrow is Independence Day. Please take a moment to think of the troops.

We had our first FISH 101 Bonuses yesterday!! Shifts A and B processed over 101,000 pounds of salmon over their shifts. Each employee will receive a $50 bonus with their first paycheck. Shift C came close, but they have to pick up the pace!

Important News:

*You must clock in at least <u>9 minutes</u> before your shift. Time Theft is a Crime!!!!!!!!

*Laundry service will be resumed tomorrow.

Fish Count: 294,000 (Not too bad, Klakers)

Weather: High of 65, clear. Sunrise—5:34 a.m. Sunset—11:36 p.m.

Alaska Word of the Day: At-Will Employment—A law meaning that an employer or employee can end employment at any time, for almost any reason. In order to maintain a nimble workforce, most US states, like Alaska, practice at-will employment.

Seventeen

Slime line days snorting accelerol and bullshitting with Bayram and thinking of ways I can push Jarrod in front of a forklift, but on the third day, or maybe the fourth, who can say, who would care, the power flickers and dies eleven hours into the shift and in the quiet and the blackness I can hear Bayram's hot sniffly breathing and HARD WORKER and girlfriend and the rest of us whispering, and Ernesto's yelling at the other end of the department and his footsteps are getting louder, loud as some kind of psycho killer, but before he can murder us, he clangs into something metal and cries SON OF A BITCH! and the laughing ripples down the line, and he's telling us to shut it, but we're not going to shut nothing, no, not in the dark, we're more than arms, or maybe less now, just voices, and we're laughing because it's all funny, right, a factory in the wilderness, a bunch of broke-ass fools cutting up fish we could never afford, and a fillet smacks the top of my head, and another wizzes past, then I can hear the rubbery zipping of Bayram's suit as he rears back and smacks me in the ass with a fillet, and I reach for him, and I tickle him, and now he's smacking me again, cackling, and more fillets are flying, and someone yells FOOD FIGHT, and I zing one Frisbee-style and hear it slap the wall behind the carni-tech, and we're all a part of something, no shit, no shit Beaver, and a generator somewhere fires up and the flood lights explode from the corners of the processor and across from me HARD WORKER is all bright eyes and teeth and he's a person, real and horny and funny and fucked-up as me, and there's so much more to this than the money and the freezer and my dad, his dangling eye, let it flutter, forgive him, and my mom, and everybody, but then Ernesto tells us to pitch the fillets in an ice tub and clock out—something major is fucked, big repairs needed—and it hits me that these next few hours are dollars I'll never get back.

Eighteen

Power's out in the chow house too and all of Kevin's maintenance guys are hurrying around saying conspiratorial shit about pipe wrenches and car batteries, and I'm heading back to the bunkhouse to try to crash when I bump into this dude Sven I know from herring. He works in the roe house now, down by the boatyard. He pilfered a flashlight on the way out the door. He has bud and wants to chill.

"Can I bring a buddy of mine?"

It's midnight but only half dark, blue like new denim, and Sven and Bayram and me walk to the boatyard and climb the shell of a big dead excavator left to rust, out onto the extended arm, ten feet off the ground, where we sit with our legs dangling like those old-time construction workers in New York photos. It'd be cool if there was someone to take our picture, hang it on the wall of a library in the future, where someone could walk by and look.

From the excavator we can see upriver to the spot where the alpenglow fizzles and dies on the mountains. Across the river, the fish shacks are lit up and downriver there's still power, too. There's a bonfire on the far beach, tiny like a matchhead. There's so much more to see, and maybe if I can make it through the season, I'll get to see some of it.

In the roe house, Sven works pulling eggs and pressing them into blocks that get salted and flash frozen. I heard it's more boring than the slime line, but Sven likes it because it's easy and because he can bullshit with the workers who deliver the roe. He's a lazy nibshit but generous with his pot. He works like a motherfucker for three, four days then sloughs off for a week and almost gets fired. His parents are historians of early Viking exploration on the Eastern Canadian coast. Sven's a good guy to know.

"Someone killed the power," he says. "All the foremen were acting like it was intentional."

"Fucking ignorant," I say. "We're gonna be way behind."

"I should have done more research," Bayram says. "I was thinking we would have mountains."

"Same," I tell him.

It's so windy we have to huddle together and open up our coats to light Sven's joint. So windy I can't smell the smoke. We're swinging our legs in metronome patterns and talking shit about work—Jarrod hit a kid with a forklift and the kid got fired—when the rap of claws on the gravel below startles me. Like a dog on linoleum, but heavier.

"Shh," Sven says, pointing.

It's a big bear, but they all look big to me. Long legged, chestnut brown, shoulders like stegosaurus plates, swaying as he walks the gravel road. He passes us, stops to sniff the air, looks up, says Whatever, and heads for the dumpster next to the mechanic's workshop at the edge the boneyard.

"I have been waiting for this," Bayram whispers.

Apparently there's still power in the workshop because the motion light trips and glows the color of piss in a bottle. The bear steps into the light. His fur's matted and dark except for one plate-sized bald patch on the side of his neck. Underneath it looks like human skin and now the white streak comes back to me. I can't rub it clear. There was this poem we read in high school about a guy who climbs into the corpse of a dead bear to survive a snowstorm, and when he comes out, he's become a bear. For a second I wish for the same, but with all of it—the bear, the light, the dumpster, the six brown boots dangling below us. Friendship? Life? I'd crawl inside this picture and die.

The bear stands and scoops a bag of trash from inside. He eats a banana peel. He eats some bread. He eats a fillet still wrapped in the plastic. He would eat my body and have no thoughts. Whose bone did I find?

"If they had thumbs," Sven says. "Look out."

"Yes," Bayram says, giggling. "Then they could carry guns."

"And text. Then they could get phones and text. Make plans. Strategize."

Sven says, "Where would they charge their phones?"

"Good point."

The steel door to the workshop flies open and a mechanic steps out.

"Dude," we holler. "Hey. Hey, dude. Bear."

The old man is silhouetted against the motion light with a cigarette glowing red from his mouth. You can see the cherry move as he turns and studies the bear. Then he walks past it, casual, chill, like the bear, closer than I'd dream of getting. "That motherfucker could eat me for breakfast," he says, walking under us. The alpenglow's gone. All that's left is the bear and the trash.

Sven whispers, "You guys want to hear something cool about the Vikings?"

He doesn't wait for an answer.

"When they wanted to wild out, before a battle, they'd put on a bear skin and eat some shrooms and *be* a bear. *Berserker* means bear shirt. They'd become the bear."

Bayram says that in Turkey, men used to collect bear cubs and force them to dance. "They would put rings in their noses," he says. "Like this." He grabs at my nose, but I swat his hand away. "And they put little chimes on their paws and bells on their legs and during festivals bears were paraded down from the mountains to dance for everyone."

The bear disappears around the far side of the dumpster. I ask if Bayram ever got to see the bears dance. He says they outlawed it years ago because it was so cruel but when he was a boy his dad took him to a sanctuary in the western part of the country where rescued bears lived in pens with nice trees where they could scratch their backs. They were obese. The sanctuary sold meat scraps, and if you waved the scraps in front of the fence, you could still get them to dance.

"Weird," Sven says. "Real Stockholm Syndrome shit."

"My father was disappointed they weren't still wearing their bells. He actually started booing the bears."

"You think that's bad? When I was seven my dad took us to Denmark to look at a pit where Vikings sacrificed their own kids."

They laugh a little and go quiet. Quiet like it's my turn.

One time my dad took us on a daytrip to the Grand Canyon of Pennsylvania. Two hours on little roads, through Main Streets with every third or fourth storefront extracted like a root canal. It was the furthest I'd been from home, but it looked mostly the same. Trees and hills, farms and gas wells. My mom brought along her Bon Jovi tapes and the two of them argued about whether Bon Jovi was too soft while I sat curled in the middle, my dad swatting me every time I stretched my legs too close to the stick shift.

The canyon was more like a narrow valley, but I didn't care. It was a long way down, endless green to the river. We were above the birds. I could see them catch the currents and blow past us. An Indian family piled out of a van with New Jersey plates and took about five hundred photographs. An Amish family piled out of a tourist van with PA plates and took none. My mom gave me a quarter for the viewfinder and stayed in the truck, smoking. Across the canyon, at the other rim, there was another overlook and I could see another kid with the viewfinder pointed as us. Soon we were snipers, howling bullets back and forth. I ducked and fired, protected my family, garnered many medals. When I turned and looked back, my dad was sitting on a wooden bench near an Amish guy in a huge hat. They were leaning toward each other, whispering about something. The man's cheeks were blood red from holding back a laugh. He was literally biting his own lip to keep it in. I said what and my dad said to mind my own business. It was like that everywhere he went. He started secret clubs that I could never join.

Quiet still. The stoned illusion of shared thoughts. Boat lights bobbing on the water downriver. What would happen if people could hear me thinking?

"Wanna hear something crazy?" I say.

They do.

The bone.

"Probably a fisherman," Sven says.

"I think it was just a bear."

"Or, you know what?" he says, whispering. "Maybe the dude from the bear house."

I shake my head at him.

"He just absconded, man. Like gone. A few years before I started here. That's why the house is still full of his shit. I think he was married to the net lady."

The Klak Fancy Letter
Wednesday, July 5th

Hello Klakers,

Shift C got a FISH 101 Bonus yesterday, while the rest of us missed out due to a malfunction at the processor. We're forecasted to have record numbers of fish in the next week. Buckle down and prepare to work your butts off.

Important News:

*Please look out for anything that seems strange or unusual at the processor. It's up to all of us to make this a safe and profitable season!

*Bears have been showing up at the processor lately. This happens every year. Please stay away from the bears!! Bears are **very** dangerous. Please be careful of your surroundings, especially at night. Stay away from dumpsters and make noise as you walk.

*Laundry service will be suspended this week while we repair some machines.

Fish Count: 280,000

Weather: High of 65, clear. Sunrise—5:27 a.m. Sunset—11:34 p.m.

Alaska Word of the Day: Mauling—Mauling is a violent attack from an animal, often a bear. Last year, 5 people were **fatally** mauled by bears in Alaska. Recently a fisherman was mauled by a juvenile bear in the boatyard and received 37 stitches in his leg and groin!

Nineteen

By morning the processor's up and running and two big Moldovan guys from the slime line are redesignated as security, strutting around the cannery grounds, holding their heavy flashlights between their legs, pulsing the button when I walk by, pretending to piss light. They're looking for something. For what? Nobody will say it outright. It was a problem with the electric, Ernesto says. Don't say shit to QC. But everybody's whispering—it was nothing, it was everything, it was a rival processor, a pissed off employee, a pissed off local, Native, white, who knows, everybody knows, they just know something different—and me? All I know is that I've got a noseful of accelerol and work to do.

We're already backed up from the power outage and now we're slammed with fish. More than we can handle, breaking processing records, earning bonuses, bonuses, bonuses. I take a bump to seventeen-hour days, baby, an extra eighty bucks a week. But then workers get poached from other processors, coming in at a higher rate than we're making, pissing everybody off, and when that still doesn't cut it, the processor hires on a half-dozen

Yup'ik women from across the river in South Klak, all teen girls except for one old woman. They fillet by hand on some white foldout tables between the slime line and the glazing machine.

They bring their own bibs. Green and black, not like ours, and duct-taped at the seams. They don't bother with hair nets and QC doesn't say shit. Even when it's crazy busy, they take full breaks. They step away from the table and stretch. They chat while they work and they barely have to even look down. Just one hard slice behind the gills, from collar to spine, a long drag of the blade following the backbone, left or right of the dorsal fin, and now the fish is open, the fish is meat, and cold fingers pry open the slit and the blade sinks deeper, and in a few seconds the fillet is free, the fish is flipped, repeat. They pluck the tiny pin bones with tweezers that chatter, trim the fat, and the fillet goes to the glazer.

I'm watching them work on my break, so lost in it that Ernesto's standing right next to me, shoulder-close, before I even notice.

"Can you fillet?" he asks me.

"No."

"It's not hard," he says. "But it's not as easy as they make it look."

"They look different than the carnitech."

"For sure," he says. "They get a better cut around the backbone than the machine gets. I tried telling them we don't need to be that careful, but if you've been doing something one way your whole life, you're not going to change for some fat Filipino."

Now the old lady's looking up at us. Her teeth are a mess and she's got deep smile lines like parenthesis around her mouth.

"Ernesto," she says. "You need something from us?"

"Yeah," he says. "Teach this little shit how to do fish."

She shoves me into the circle of girls and mid-sentence their conversation flips to Yup'ik—a string of C's and Q's and long, low U's. But I can still tell gossip when I hear it. I heard it in Turkish this morning, Romanian in the afternoon, and now it's the same. They're talking about the power outage.

"You know how?" the girl across the table says.

They're using their own ulus, these half-moon-shaped knives that rock across the table. I take the only flat knife and a bright silver sockeye and I mostly get the collar cut right, but things go bad when I make the first cut along the backbone. It's hard to even say how it goes so wrong, but I just keep at it until the old lady puts her hand across mine and tells me to stop.

"That poor salmon," she says. "Swam a thousand miles just to be murdered with an axe!"

Giggling—

"Show me?"

"No," she says. "Just watch."

Just watch—the star of light on the edge of the knife blade. The blood crawling toward the table edge. The way the girl across from me flings a fish head and it spins four times and stops, facing me. Little teeth, white mouth, one green eye staring up, and now it's my eye and I see myself all distorted and sick and I remember looking across the river at the fish camps a few weeks ago and telling Bonnie I felt so *bad* for everybody over there, so *sorry* for them, and she scolded me about the uselessness of my pity, and it hits me that maybe they feel sorry for me. This dipshit spending summer inside and he can't even cut up a fish. I'm watching and wondering when Ernesto comes back and says if I'm not gonna get anything done I can go back to the slime line.

"He's fine," the woman says. "He's doing just fine."

And when Ernesto nods and turns away, she asks me how I liked working with Bonnie, and I realize I owe the net lady another favor.

Twenty

The next day, the women are gone.

I stand there before my shift looking at the empty patch of concrete where the fillet tables were and I'm feeling grateful and sad and dogshit tired. Where'd they even go?

"Home," Ernesto says. "They wanted more money."

Back on the line with all the other little trolls. Just gnawing at salmon. It's so easy it's hard, standing there with pinched shoulders and fingers curling in toward the palm. We've all been swapping foreign germs and there's this relentless, wet hacking on the slime line. The bathroom feels the pressure first. The constant septic reek. The way there's never enough toilet paper. Good news for me is that accelerol makes it impossible to shit. It's like I'm keeping it all in storage. On the line my body leans forward. A falling feeling. When my eyes open, HARD WORKER and his girlfriend are laughing at me.

He says, "Americans sleep standing."

She says, "Just like cattle."

———

Every three hours for the next three days—

Accelerol and coffee and a bran muffin on break.

Flashlight Moldovans pacing the processor grounds.

Accelerol and coffee and a bran muffin on break.

QC with his clipboard, sniffing around.

Accelerol and coffee and a bummed cigarette on break.

Bayram says he's going to bill me at the end of the season.

He taps his temple and it sounds like a piggy bank jingling.

(Sometimes it's hard to know what's real.)

The Moldovans are looking at us.

Bayram thinks they're watching him.

Does Jarrod know I'm watching him?

I treat that motherfucker like homework.

Facts—he eats bran muffins and only smokes half a cigarette at a time.

Facts—he forges fish temps in the logbooks.

Facts—he never rinses his break room mug.

Facts—he sits with the supervisors in the chow house.

Facts—he's always talking to the Moldovan guys with the flashlights.

Accelerol and coffee and I take his mug from the break room and dip my balls in it.

Accelerol and coffee and, oh, shit, that wasn't his mug after all.

(My bad, Javier!)

Accelerol and coffee and, oh, shit, this bottle's empty.

"Are you even listening?"

Bayram's sitting across from me in the chow house, telling me about his dad, who lost his job as the lighting technician at Ankara's famous opera house after missing a lighting change because he was busy kissing an understudy half his age. He'd been showering her with gifts for two years and now the family finances are a mess and Bayram's taking a break from business school to help straighten them out.

Bayram's beard is slowly climbing up his cheeks and the unibrow he must trim at home is on the attack. I see it advancing a little every day, and it's made more obvious by the way he exaggerates his facial expressions so I can hear him over the line. He's like a living emoji when he tells me about his plan. iPods. They're crazy expensive in Turkey because of trade regulations and exchange rates and it's impossible to get a refurbished one. He's going to order them here with his processor money and take them to Turkey to resell. Then, he'll parlay that money into more iPods to resell, which he can flip for more iPods to sell. He's got a spreadsheet about it and everything. With that money, maybe, hopefully, he can help his mother move to Istanbul, nearer to his sister.

His Turkish friends have basically ditched him, moving to the other end of the slime line, blocking him from his seat at the chow house so he's had to slink over to our table and find room at the end. He says his friends feel "deceived" by him. They want the referral money the processor gave him for bringing in new workers: fifty bucks for each friend. He says he didn't deceive shit. He came in as blind as them. I'm not so sure.

Right now, they're scowling at him from their table on the other side of the chow house. He's sitting opposite me, gulping his Swiss Miss from a chipped coffee mug. When one of them yells something in Turkish, he winces.

"They found out about some of my business plans," he says. "They are angry that I didn't tell them."

"So you did it?"

"Yes," he says. "I had to go to Klak to find internet access. Then I saw that police officer outside of the library, but I did it. Nineteen refurbished iPods, arriving in two weeks."

"Go big or go home."

"Go big *and* go home," he says. He reaches into his hoodie pocket and slides two cupped hands across the table.

"A gift."

Two small clementines, just starting to pucker, tiny green bruises spreading from the stem. Bright orange, the color of road cones or rain gear. They look so out of place with our eggs and salmon and rice. They look proud to be here, proud of how far they've come. When I squint I can practically see the fingerprints of everyone who ever touched them. Pickers and sorters and QC and I don't even know who else. Too perfect to eat, no way, I want to just put them in a shadowbox and stare.

"How did you get these?"

He just winks. Turks are always winking. After a while, you just get used to it. I put them in my pocket for later.

Now his Turkish friends are calling for him across the room.

"They're making a petition," he says. "Demanding the same pay as the workers hired later. They want me to get some Americans to sign it."

I look back down to the fruit, think through it.

"No way."

Twenty-One

"Yo, Sven!"

He's walking over the dunes to the boneyard alone to smoke weed on the old excavator at the end of his shift. It's morning and I'm on my last break and his shadow's long behind him on the sand, like a net I could grab and reel in to shake the pills from. The tide must be up because the air smells clean and salty and the birds are all chilling way up by the dumpsters at the plant.

"Hey," he says. "You see this shit?" It's a quarter piece of notebook paper that says, DO YOU WANT FAIRER PAY? MEETING 4 PM OUTSIDE CHOW HOUSE.

Bayram. Jesus fucking Christ, Bayram.

"You have anything to do with this?" he says.

"Fuck no," I say. "Why?"

"Just thought you might," he says. "It's like signing a piece of paper saying *fire me*."

"I need some more of those trucker pills. I'm dogshit today."

"I'm out."

"Damn," I say. "Catch up later."

And I'm halfway up the dune before he yells, "Hey. I got a buddy whose got something pretty similar."

The Klak Fancy Letter
Saturday, July 8th

Hello Klakers,

This is a strange message to write.

I have been informed by our QC Expert Nigel that some salmon fillets appear to have been sabotaged within the processor. **It looks as if they have pieces bitten out of them!!!!**

Clearly, this is happening before the salmon reach the packing department as it would be impossible to bite pieces out of frozen fillets.

I don't know what kind of sick degenerate would think this is funny, but know that it is not.

Imagine what this would do to our reputation? You will be caught and prosecuted!

Important News:

*There have been some reports of valuables going missing in the bunk-houses. We're looking into it. Please remember that Klak Fancy is not responsible for the loss or theft of your personal property.

Fish Count: 287,000. (So close, guys!!!!!)

Weather: High of 66 (warm!) clear. Sunrise—5:30 a.m.
Sunset—11:31 p.m.

Alaska Word of the Day: Anisakid Nematodes—Anisakid nematodes, or cod worms, are a dangerous parasite that lives in raw salmon. Flash-freezing kills these parasites, which is how people safely eat sushi. To bite into a raw fillet before flash-freezing is to risk serious illness.

Twenty-Two

We eat summer-camp style, packed together on long wooden benches, elbows bumping, feet touching, spilled food everywhere, just fuel, nobody cares about shit except for getting the seats at the edge so you don't have to thread your XTRATUFs between the bench and table. Most days, we're that tired.

Bayram sits down next to me with his hood up over his face, trying to hide his black eye. His buddies? He doesn't want to talk about it. The meeting? He says don't worry about it. The petitions? Mind your own business. Can I help? I can leave it alone, he says. So I do.

Next to me on the other side there's Sven and next to Sven there's Penn, who goes to U Penn and never lets you forget it. Then there's Tennessee from Tennessee and Nate, a vegan from California who only bathes in apple cider vinegar and always gives a different reason why. Almost across from me, the evil Jarrod Haverberger sits down. Everybody on his side scoots to give him room. I hate that.

Next to Jarrod there's Smitty, a big metalhead from Iowa with long red hair. He knew all about the yaba that Sven got me. Said rickshaw drivers in Thailand use it. Said it's like meth, but medical. Safe! He's telling us how he got to Klak Fancy.

"It started with Hootie and the Blowfish," he's saying, "and ended up with some car keys." Smitty rooms in the bunkhouse on the cot next to mine. I've heard the story before.

"Listen to this, Bay," I say. "Hootie and the Blowfish is a band."

"I know," he says, and winks.

"I had this girlfriend," Smitty says. "And she was obsessed with Hootie and the Blowfish. She had one of the singer's T-shirts that she bought at a charity thing. Anyway, she and this friend of hers made a weekend out of seeing them. And she came home, walked in the door, and just flat out said, 'I sucked Darius Rucker's dick.'"

"Wait," Sven says. "Is that the singer?"

"Yes."

"Then who is Hootie?"

"That was my fucking question," Smitty says. "She said, 'I sucked Darius Rucker's dick' and I said 'Who's that?' She weaseled into an after party, got drunk, and next thing she knew she was sucking his dick in the bathroom of a Ramada Inn. She didn't even apologize, just laid it out there. They're not even popular anymore! So I was mad about it for a few days, but a dick's just a dick, you know? It's not like she brought it home with her. So I said Fine. Just no more Hootie when I'm around. She said okay. But I'd catch her listening to it and we'd fight and she'd promise to stop. Then Hootie came to Des Moines.

That was the end of it. I drew the line and she jumped right over it."

Sven leans across the table, puts his hand over Smitty's and says, "And how does that make you feel?"

"Hold up," Smitty says. "One night at a party, a few nights after she left, I was all fucked up and some guy passed me a meth bubbler. You ever try that shit? Anyway I went on a bender and ended up giving some dude a ride home from a party and I take him way out of town to some old ass place in a bean field and when we pull in, the motherfucker says, 'Alright. Give me your wallet.'"

"And I was like Oh Hell No."

"And he reaches over and pulls the keys from the ignition and tosses them out of the car window and he's like 'Come on man. Just give it up. Please.'"

"He actually said please?"

"The motherfucker said Please as he was trying to rob me. So I got out of the car and I said 'Let's do it.' And we did. He got out and beat my ass for fourteen dollars. I was just laying on the ground screaming *Help* and he just took the money and jogged down the road. I found my keys, started the car, and you know what the fuck comes on the radio?"

He clears his throat like he's planning to sing.

We wait.

Instead, he whispers, "That one where he cries over the Dolphins."

Dolphins! His fat fists pound the table and shake loose the feeling of fall-apart laughter. It swells and I can feel the happy chemicals it gives me, laughing with these guys, and when we idle down, Sven asks why you'd get your ass kicked over fourteen dollars. Bayram says it's a matter of pride. Penn says you risked a lot more than fourteen bucks in that fight. Smitty says it was his last fourteen bucks, though! That was the real kicker. He didn't even have enough money for gas to get home.

Jarrod says, "The fuck's wrong with you guys? I'd rather die than hand over my wallet." He's not even laughing. He's mad we even think this is funny.

I say, "It's fourteen bucks. You can't buy shit with fourteen bucks."

Bayram says, "It's just an hour of overtime work. Think about it like that."

Jarrod says, "That's classic beta mentality."

"Says the laziest motherfucker here."

Jarrod reaches across the table and flips over my tray with his long middle finger. The coffee cup hits the floor and shatters. Water running through the table slats, wet legs, eggs in my lap, rice down my shirt, on my face, in my hair. Fear and rage in double doses and nobody does anything to help me. He's the nephew of the big boss. The muscles are just the bonus. Jarrod. Even his stillness is smug. There's a bite of B-Grade salmon on his fork, fatty and bruised, hanging a few inches from his mouth. Shame—I don't know which one of us to murder first. I say something like what the fuck man but my voice circles back to me, thin, and weak, and young, like a kid, trembling. Everybody in the chow house is watching.

Jarrod says, "Say you're sorry."

"Fuck off." And now my eyes are getting wet and Jarrod drops his head so our eyes meet. He already knows how this will go. It's gone this way his whole life.

"Just say it."

Twenty-Three

Before he flipped my tray, Jarrod was an abstract thing to
hate. Something far off, like war. But now this shit's right in
front of me. I can touch it. I can smell its sour breath. Jarrod.
He's like a ghost turned flesh and blood. Or a disease, a
humiliating one like syphilis or suicide. I feel infected when I
think about him, laying in his cot, enjoying his good night's
rest, dreaming about cage fighting or being able to count or
whatever. Jarrod has his own shack, like the supervisors. His
is along the footpath past the shower house and Helen's
shack, next to the thick alders between the grounds and the
bear house. It's after 2 a.m., dark as it gets, and it seems like
he's asleep.

Even getting here's been a master class in hustle and
shame. Earlier, at shift change, I stopped Ernesto on my way to
the line. "Bad news, boss," I said, puckering my lips.

"I got the shits."

He squinted. "You look fine."

I said, "You want fucking evidence?"

Ernesto looked down the line. Workers slipping on their yellow rubber gloves and HARD WORKER was rubbing his girlfriend's left hand, looking up at her tired, sad face.

"I can't lose you today," he said. "We're about to be fucking slammed."

"I'm here. Just advance notice for when I run off the line trying to hold my asshole shut."

"Do your best."

For the first hour I made these little head-shaking motions like maybe there was water in my ears, followed by a few well-timed grabs at my stomach. Eventually when the line was stalled I ran to the bathroom and I did it again forty-five minutes later, and again an hour after that. Each time I hollered SORRY ERNESTO and waddled across the factory floor.

On break, I skipped my muffin and laid flat on a break room bench clutching my stomach. Ernesto walked by and slapped me lightly with his gloves. He asked if I was going to live and I said if I died, I'd die fighting. He laughed and gave me an accelerol. Stack that shit with yaba and you'll see in four dimensions.

Between break and dinner I ran to the bathroom two more times. Once I cut in front of the forklift, screaming BATHROOM EMERGENCY so that everyone in fish house would see me.

Hahaha, motherfuckers.

After dinner, Jarrod's shift switched out while mine stayed on. Two hours after that, between breaks, I approached Ernesto clutching my stomach and screwing up my face. We were on pace for the FISH 101 Bonus and Ernesto had gone so hoarse screaming that when he opened his mouth no sounds came out. But he was shaking his head No.

"I have some meds in the bunkhouse," I told him.

He looked down the line. "Can it wait?"

I said, "Don't you say a goddamn word but I need to change my underwear too."

He said to hurry, slapped on some gloves, and took my place on the line.

Now the hood's up on my bear shirt but I'm not going full-ass berserk, no, I'm calm. I'm in total control. I skulk. I creep. I fucking prowl past the shower house until I find the spot. Each shack is just that—a pallet floor with walls built up, knock-kneed windows, recycled tin roof. Aside from the privacy, and the status, they're not much better than a bunkhouse. But that's what they offer, something to claim as your own. The shacks are powered with extension cords that run back to a main box with outlets, like a slum in a spy movie. It's not hard to trace Jarrod's back and pull the plug. Maybe he has a plug-in alarm clock. Everyone in the bunkhouse does. This won't be enough, but maybe something. It'll be a start. I can see him oversleeping, a no-show at the start of the shift. I'll get pulled to replace him. From there, I'll forge some logbooks from the last shift and point out to QC how bad he's fucked up the freezers. Maybe then this femur will disappear from the corner of my eye.

I'm heading back when I hear the branches break. My arm hairs quill. Moose. But then the unmistakable huff and snort.

The heavy, heavy pant. The sound of size, power, a no-fucks-given sound. He's behind me, past the shacks, somewhere in the dark alders, rooting, and does he even know I'm there? The bushes shake. He's getting closer. I'm supposed to make noise, clap and address the bear. *Hey Bear, Hello Bear. Hi Bear.* But bear safety ain't designed for sabotage missions. Slowly, and lowly, I trace the extension cord back to Jarrod's shack and crouch by his closed door where at least I can hide if I have to. Inside I can hear him snoring. Insane fantasies—Jarrod opens the shack door to the screaming, the claws and teeth, my insides outside. I hope it scars him for life. I hope he's maimed in the escape. I become cannery lore, a legend, my picture on the wall of the Black Dog. Who is Joe? Who is Garrett? Time does its thing and then I hear, far off, *Get Going, Bear*, and the sound of rocks banging against a dumpster.

Just as I'm standing to leave I see Jarrod's boots tucked under the eave by the door.

Like a spasm, I remember this time when I was like ten, home "sick," cruising around the trailer court in the rain on my Huffy. It's spring, warm, and that fresh rain smell rises from the pavement. This is my new Huffy, painted the color of a bruise, blue fading to green. It sparkles. It shines. It's mine.

From our trailer, near the field at the back of the court, I ride the main loop past the house where Nick and Natalie Destin live and past the Patels' house. Their mom hangs their clothes on a line in the yard and I like the way the colors buck and flap in the wind. Past the Patels', I circle toward the old-school single-wides at the far back of the park, past the lady that hands out whole cans of pop if you'll also take a pocket bible, and past the two silver campers where the ropey guys have new motorcycles and new girlfriends every couple of months.

I bike up the big hill past mom's friend Randy's trailer. My mom told me I'm supposed to go say thanks for the bike. Outside, under his eave, Randy snubs his cigarettes half-smoked in a coffee can full of sand. Sometimes Nick Destin and I pilfer the butts to smoke in the woods. One time he burned his eyelashes lighting one and had to bribe his sister to doll him up with mascara. He said if I told anyone he'd beat my ass.

I round the corner and start down the big hill. It's raining harder now and when I pull the brakes, they squeal, a baby animal sound, but I'm barely slowing down, the sharp curve by our trailer coming, and a truck taking the curve, heading my way.

I put a foot down onto the pavement to catch some friction like I always do. But this time it's different. My shoe grabs something in the road, sends it hard into my heel. I hit the soft gravel, the grass, the railroad-tie parking block in front of the trailer. The world flips, it spins, and my Huffy cartwheels into the trailer. I try to stand. There's a nail sticking out of my shoe. I kick the shoe off with the other foot and now the heel of my sock is turning pink.

Inside the phone is dead. Just silence on the other end of the receiver. My foot's starting to feel like I've sat on it for too long. I check the phone again but the phone is still dead. I put on some slippers, hobble to the neighbors in the rain, and they call my mom at work.

On the other end of the line, I can hear her say, "Fuckity fuckity fuckity fuck."

Later, after a tetanus shot, we bring home Little Caesar's and Coke in red cans. My mom scrubs the blood from the carpet. She's worried about the security deposit. She's mad I was out riding my bike in the rain. Don't I know how that makes her look? Couldn't she trust me at all? And the phone. Too many pesky telemarketers and she forgot to plug it back in. It was years before I figured out that *pesky telemarketer* was code for my dad.

Now, Jarrod's XTRATUFs. They're practically brand new.

When you know what you want, there are no hard decisions. Only what needs to be done and what doesn't. This is clear to me in the same way that everything else is becoming clear. When it gets late in my shift I can see the long arc of my life. I'm wading out of the ooze of my parents, shedding my bullshit like afterbirth. Soon I'll be the finished version. What I mean is that if I could be any animal I would be a fish. If I could be any inanimate object it would be a fillet knife. If I could be any person I would be my own true self. The person I'll be.

Let me say it better—I sneak to the shower house, pop some aluminum skirting from the steps, quiet the rattling, swallow down the pills bragging inside my heart, pry a nail from the skirting, take it back to Jarrod's shack, kiss it for good luck and Godspeed, thank it for its service, and wedge it into the heel of his boot so that the tip just breaks through the insole. It's a roofing nail. All that's left was a quarter inch. More-or-less. Maybe more.

More.

Oh, fuck yes—think of the second when surprise becomes pain, when pain becomes recognition, when hopefully Jarrod will wonder if this is a payback, if not literally then at least on the karmic level?

When I hear coughing from an open shack window I break into a run, the sour-candy-taste of revenge, and I round the corner to the shower house and run into Bonnie carrying three grocery bags and a pipe wrench the length of her arm. When she hits the ground, salmon roll out from her bag.

"What in the fuck are you doing?" she says.

"What in the fuck are *you* doing?" I say.

I don't stop. I don't help her up. I keep running, straight into the plant and through the boot dip and I'm still panting when I accept Ernesto's verbal shellacking without even the tiniest trace of evidence in my smile. He says he sent someone to my bunkhouse to check on me.

"I was in the bathroom," I tell him. "Whatever just happened in my guts was diabolical."

Back on the line and I notice for the first time how much the fillets look like a trail of bloody footprints.

Twenty-Four

We're so slammed for the rest of the shift that Ernesto splits up our breaks into groups of two to keep from shutting down the line for even a minute. Bayram and I take our break at sunup, standing on the concrete patio behind the break room in the scattered rain with our rubber bibs pulled down to the hips so that the top half hangs down like the tails of slugs. Bayram eats a muffin with raisins that look like dead horseflies and I drink coffee with two packs of Swiss Miss swirled in it. Revenge, cocoa, exhaustion—it's the little things.

Sunrise on one side and a touch of northern lights the other way, the color of spilled Mountain Dew. A funny thing about the view from the cannery is it's different each way you look. You turn your head, raw river. Graveyard for boats. Trailer park. Spongy taiga. The village with its ass kicked by the wind. If you were a photographer, you could make it seem like you'd been all sorts of places. This is the best I've felt in a very long time.

He says, "We got thirty-seven signatures demanding to be paid when we stay past the shift. Zep thinks we're losing maybe an hour a week or more. Plus we want the same rate as the workers that came later."

"You're going to get in trouble. The season's not long enough for this shit."

He laughs. "Me? I can say the same thing about you."

"What do you mean?"

"I spent most of my youth pretending to be ill. Not your best performance."

I nod. "I was hoping Ernesto would just let me off early. I'm just so beat."

"I see." He pulls a hunk from his muffin. The rain is turning the sunrise a funny wet color over the bluffs on the opposite side of the river. A tart color, dripping pink, slurpable. Will it taste bitter to be back in the freezer?

I say, "Wait. Why were you always faking sick?"

"What are you studying again?"

"Psychology," I say. "One semester left."

"Psychology is interesting to you, yeah? Why?"

I say, "Because the bathroom ceiling when I was a kid had this textured paint on it. And I used to lay in the bathtub and come up with these crazy fucking stories about all the things I saw in the textures. A horse with hands, a couple of dragons. A lady pushing a stroller, a cop that rode a cheetah. A guy with two dicks. A fish with the head of a . . ."

"What in the hell is that?"

A little red fox, skulking out from the alders, mangy and snake-like, probably one of the ones that dens under the roe house. You can see the bones they scattered at the den's hole, the smooth dirt where they slink under the joists. The foxes know when it's break time. Sometimes one will be waiting when you walk out.

I say, "You've never seen him? It's a fox."

"A fox?" he tries to place the word.

"It's like a little wolf."

"Very little. Do they make good pets?"

"Let's see." I toss a piece of muffin into the gravel road and the fox darts out and grabs it and scrams. Part of his tail is bare from mange, a poodle poof at the end. Bay tosses some muffin and now he eats in the open, his eyes blooming in the flood lights. Each crumb Bay tosses brings the fox a little closer. You can see his mind at work, fighting with itself, weighing the risk and reward.

"I bet he'd take it from your hand," I whisper.

Bayram leans back on the bench and stretches his arm far behind him with the huge muffin in his palm. A minute passes. The fox lunges, chickens out, tries again. And as the cannery door bangs open the fox is running down the road with the muffin in his jaws and his tail bouncing behind him.

The Klak Fancy Letter
Sunday, July 9th

Hello Klakers,

Something strange is going on at my processor, and I won't stand for it!

More salmon were discovered with what appears to be **human bite marks**. If you have any information about this, or if you see any suspicious behavior at the processor—including unauthorized visitors or workers in unusual places—please alert your supervisor. You will be rewarded.

Important News:

*Remember that Klak Fancy is drug and alcohol free. Buying, selling, or possessing illegal drugs is a cause for termination.

*With the season at its peak, bonuses are attainable every day, if your shift has the guts for it.

Fish Count: 367,000 (SOOO Close to our Lifetime Record!!!)

Weather: High of 57, rainy. Sunrise—5:32 a.m. Sunset—11:29 p.m.

Alaska Word of the Day: Retention Bonus—A retention bonus is a payout from an employer to an employee if they stay at a job for a certain length of time. In your case, your retention bonus is your room and board, which is provided free of charge if you sufficiently finish the season with us. If not, the bonus is revoked and fees are subtracted from your earnings.

Twenty-Five

When I see Helen in the freezer suit, I know. I know my plan worked because I can't see Jarrod's idiot face on the packing floor. I know that she's wearing my freezer suit because of the duct-taped knee, and I know that it'll still be warm from her body when I slip it on. She's standing by the strip curtain between the slime line and packing with her hands interlocked on her head and the suit unzipped down to the waist, black hoodie underneath. The suit's too big, the cuffs folded over, and she looks dogshit tired.

I say, "You get demoted too?"

"I just pulled six hours of surprise freezer work." She drops her arms, lets them swing. "After my twelve."

The banana army is walking behind us and taking their spots on the slime line. Bayram passes, slows, and pokes me in the ribs. He drops a glove and takes forever to pick it up. Is he spying on me? I ask Helen what's up.

She says, "Is that one of the petition kids? Talk to him about that so I don't have to."

"Sure."

"You're a lucky fucker," she says. "You're back in the freezers. I'll need you to go back through the logs from the last week and fix them too. Just fudge the numbers. Jarrod had them all fucked up and I didn't even notice."

"Did he move departments?" Bay's still watching us.

She says, "Get to work."

So I do.

Fish come, go.

A perfect pink haze of them.

Helen is on my back for the next three days because the packing crew's always behind, fixing Jarrod's mistakes and handling the biggest run of fish the plant's ever seen. We chase the bonus back in early from the break room, and we get it. Every day we break processing records until they offer some of us a bump up to eighteen-hour days. I take the bump and days pass like a bird might. Just something you see. Just a collection of the stuff you see, the stuff you do. You see a packing worker cut his thumb half off with a box knife. You see a fillet with the tip of a knife stuck in it but you miss it on the line, and it's gone. You see a pattern on the frost in the freezer that looks like a gaping mouth. Another that looks like antlers. You see your dad in the faces of men but you never see the face of your mom and you don't want to ask yourself why. So don't, Garrett. You dumb motherfucker. Drink this shit up because soon it'll end.

Two weeks? Three?

And then?

Shut up, Garrett.

In the break room you mix your coffee with a half packet of Swiss Miss, just for the sugar. Savor that. You start smoking because you deserve it, just because Fuck You. That's Why. You start popping more yaba and palmfuls of aspirin that Ernesto gives you anytime you complain of a headache or a footache or the shits. Everything hurts. You really do get the shits. Your bowels must be karmic. The Polish girls stand on the toilet seats when they pee and so you have to wipe off the slime and scales first. Sometimes you chill in the bathroom and soak your hands in the hot water. Everyone does it. You deserve it. Savor it. Because the next day, they turn off the hot water.

You wait for the sweet joy that work brings. It's so sweet you could fuck it. Usually it shows ten hours into the shift when the yaba is kicking and the coffee is kicking and you start working faster. You jump up and down to stay warm. You hop. You sing. You carve your name into the freezer ice with a screwdriver. Every person in the cannery becomes so fucking interesting you could just kiss them. You have no brain, really. You're a maniac. You're dumb as a hound. You'd probably eat dog food if someone put it in front of you, which makes sense because you eat like a dog. You practically snort that shit, bread and something resembling a vegetable and salmon in every meal. Around you people are talking. Sometimes they're asking questions. You can tell because of how they stare, waiting. LOOK—Bayram tilting his head like a hungry dog.

He says, "Are you okay?"

He says, "You did something to him, no?"

He says, "Why are your teeth chattering?"

He says, "Another petition. Will you sign?"

He says, "What if we walked out for higher pay?"

You go outside for the last ten minutes of your break to let the sun feel you up. You lean against the warm tin wall of the chow house in a plastic lawn chair, but not the cracked one that pinches your ass, and you smoke and taste the sun-through-your-eyelids yellow. You sleep or maybe toy with sleep until a door slams and a man leaves the processor and walks past, strutting, all muscles and hair, and is he your father?

Who is Joe?

Breaks are the worst.

Did someone just say *walk out*?

Inside, break's over, and you ask Helen if she has accelerol but she says, "No. Why?"

So you ask Ernesto and he gives you two.

"Beaver," he says. "You look like shit."

Fun fact—Beavers eat their own shit. They got no choice. It takes two passes to get any vitamins out of bark. That's an example of goal-oriented behavior. That spot in my eye is getting worse. It's definitely a bone. A femur, specifically. No worries, look forward, shift's over, and I pile my tray and sit down at the bench in the chow house and Sven and Smitty are talking. I'm having a hard time making sense of others but it might just be the noise from my rocket ship carrying me to salary.

"Shit was nasty," Sven's saying. "The dude in this video had an Ichabod Crane dick."

"So, like there was no head?" Smitty says.

"No, man." Sven frowns. "The horseman was headless. Ichabod Crane was just tall and super skinny."

"And pale," I say. "Wasn't Ichabod Crane really pale?"

I look at Bayram. "Are you planning something?"

"What?" He's cramming powdered eggs into his mouth.

"You were saying something about walking out."

Chewing. The skin below his eyes is baggy and purple. He says, "I don't know what you are talking about."

"Don't fuck this up for us."

"Why are you talking so fast? You're losing it."

"Yeah," Sven says. "It's like you can breathe through your nose while you're in the middle of words."

"You could probably play the didgeridoo," Smitty says.

"Or maybe you could be a white rapper."

"You're, like, the new Eminem."

"Aren't you from a trailer park, too?"

"Have you ever tried beatboxing?"

"Or you could be auctioneer."

"Have you ever seen a speech therapist?"

"And those words you make up."

They are all smiling with big keyboard teeth.

What are you fucking losers trying to spell?

Later, I swing open the blast freezer door and see snow circulating in the long tube, frozen light in the empty space. The cold tunnel to hell, the end of the season, no fish. The big empty future is talking at me. It says *I will eat the sun*. Or maybe it's *son*. Way down at the far end, a few dozen racks of salmon are all there is. I close the door and check the other freezers, each about half-full. At the slime line I checked the fish counters. Low.

"Helen," I say. She's looking at some papers on a clipboard and has a new pale pink bandana on her head. "Did the tender miss the tide?"

"No," she says. "It didn't."

"That's a very nice bandana."

She adjusts it on her head. "Just like a newborn, wearing pink so people will know I'm a girl. Do you have any cigarettes?"

I pat my pockets, even though I know I don't. I try to will them into existence. Yaba makes many things possible. My mom called it manifesting. There's something long and hard in my chest pocket. There is a bone in my pocket. There is a pen in my pocket. Wouldn't it be nice to pull a cigarette from my pocket and give it to Helen?

"What were we talking about?"

"The fish just aren't coming in right now. If anyone asks, do me a favor and say it's normal. It's not a big deal, in the grand scheme of things."

"How grand of a scheme do you mean?"

"For some people it will be a somewhat big deal."

"But not for me?"

"No, Beaver," she says. She smiles in a very sincere way. "I need you around."

"But not normal?"

"In the Yukon, almost no salmon. In Southeast, mostly just pinks. No kings, hardly any coho. But we're getting crazy runs. Then, they just stop."

I shake my head yes.

"Never mind," she says. Her mouth slowly flips 180 degrees so that she is frowning. She has something pink between her teeth.

"What's that in your mouth?"

What's that in your eye?

Which one of us is even talking?

The Klak Fancy Letter
Saturday, July 15th

Hello Employees,

It seems like our **huge** first run of sockeye is slowing a bit, which is a good thing for you all! We might have a few shorter days in the coming week. (Fish often comes in waves like this.) I'm excited for everyone to recharge and rest up so we can make another push and get through this season!!!

Important News:

*We will be offering a $500 bonus to any information related to the person who has been biting pieces from raw salmon fillets.

Fish Count: 147,000 (We have a long way to go to make FISH 101 for each shift!!!)

Weather: High of 67 (so warm this summer!). Sunrise—5:42 a.m. Sunset—11:21 p.m.

Alaska Word of the Day: Risk—A situation exposing yourself to a potential loss. Commercial fishing is high-risk, but also high-reward.

Twenty-Six

Laying in my cot listening to the music my mind's making, just jamming, man, composing this shit in real-time.

Accelerol, accelerated—
Accelerol is over-rated!
Yaba, yaba, hey!
Yaba, yaba, hey, hey!

"Beaver," Smitty grunts. "Shut the fuck up, man."

Super sweaty or maybe I just peed a little, sometimes it happens you know, and I throw on some pants and wander down to the boatyard in the dark. Windless, cloudless, weatherless, and my skin's real tingly and hot, and suddenly the season's over, and I've been asked to stay, and I got my own little shack, Jarrod's shack, decorated with stuff I find down at the point in the low tide—bones and shells and boat parts and buoys—and I'm on the porch of my shack, looking across the river, and somehow the river's gotten small, like a Pennsylvania stream, and the women who taught me to fillet are standing on the shore, holding chalkboards, and in the boatyard I hear footsteps, and my shack's been stolen from me, and isn't it obvious that whoever got Jarrod will get me too, and across the river the women are gasping and cupping their mouths because they can see what I can't, they can see the killer behind me, the one who flipped my dad from the balcony, his footsteps are louder, the knife glints, there's nowhere to go but over the quay wall, down to the muddy river bank where they keep the bones, headfirst, I dive, Oh Shit, Oh Beaver, just keep gnawing, gnawing for fresh air in the mud.

Twenty-Seven

Last night was a little fuck-up. Sometimes when I stack Benadryl with yaba I start to hear things, okay? Some of the things I hear make sense because I'm the one saying them. Like when I start to backslide, thinking about my dad, about Bonnie, about femurs, I say, Garrett Deaver you were once a worthless boy pissing in hampers drunk in the dorms of a Pennsylvania budget university. You were once a little trailer park scudder with a knockoff Nike hoodie. You used to be the one with the nail in his foot. You used to live inside your own heart. Dead things used to make you sick. And then you got this job, Garrett. This job and these fish and this bottle of yaba from Sven.

My God I'm starving. I want to eat the whole world but I can't exercise control, exercise being the key word here because my mind is a muscle and sometimes it spasms. When this season ends—

I just don't know.

One time I came home from fourth grade and found all our plates and bowls broken on the kitchen floor. Coffee cups, beer mugs, the wedding china that never left the cabinet. The shards rippling out from the center of the floor. I thought about rocks and ponds. The shape of rage and radiation. My dad was leaning against the kitchen counter with a beer in his hand.

"Your mother dropped some dishes," he said. "Get the broom." He stood there drinking while I swept up. When he finished his bottle, he set it on the floor and gently kicked it into the pile of broken dishes. "Your mother acts like she doesn't know me at all. I'm a lot of things, but a liar isn't one of them."

I'm thinking about those broken dishes now on the beach near the quay, where a few thousand salmon spread across the dark sand. They look like shards. The air's thick with an oily fresh fish smell. In the darkness past the truck headlights, you can hear fish slapping their tails on the sand. It sounds wet and desperate, like sex.

"You're gonna pick the fuckers up," Ernesto's saying. "Put them in totes. We'll unload them in fish house and bring you back the empty truck."

He says, "Beaver, you're in charge," and he leaves.

The hose that sucks the fish from the tender blew fifty feet up from the dock and by the time they got it shut down, a few thousand fish spilled. Ernesto thinks the tender operator and the processor operator both turned the wrong valve at the same time. He said that dumbfucks have an incredible way of finding each other. He called them different ends of the same turd.

I pick my way through the fish to the edge of the concrete quay wall that keeps the river at bay. The tide's running and the tender's leaving with it, just cat eyes in the dark. On the flats below the wall where I wallowed last night, a dozen salmon are flopping around. I watch one shimmy from puddle to puddle, searching for water. It hits the river, wriggles, Peace.

They sent Sven from the roe house and when Ernesto dragged me from the freezers, he'd told me to grab someone from the line to help. I'd picked Bayram. Now we're half blind under the yellow truck lights. We mound the fish into piles, then put the piles into totes.

"I have good news," Bayram says.

"Tell me you got laid."

"As of four days ago, I am even."

Sven says, "And Garrett's fucking odd."

"No," he says. "My first paycheck covered my plane ticket, boots, and gear. The second will cover the recruitment fees, with extra. I'm officially making money."

"Yikes, man." Sven grabs two fish and slaps them together. "So if the season ended tomorrow you'd make like two-hundred bucks for the whole summer?"

"That's what I have been trying to tell everyone," he says. "I have done the math. The processor can't find new workers so quickly. They will have to negotiate with us."

"Remember I warned you," Sven says.

"I tried to tell him, too."

Sven says, "Why not go work in the EU or something?"

Sven looks at me. "The EU's like an alignment between most of the countries in Europe."

"I know what the fucking EU is, asshole."

Bayram says, "Mountains and money. That's what the recruiter kept saying. Maybe I heard mountains *of* money."

Just then, Helen comes jogging down from the plant. I can tell it's her because of all the stuff jingling on her belt. She opens the truck door and kills the headlights we've been using to work. "What the fuck is this?"

"The hose blew."

"And what the fuck is this?" She's panting and it's dark all around us. "The fish?"

"Ernesto told us pick them up and take them to the tank."

Now she's heaving fish over the quay and they're dropping with a wet thud like that bone. "You fucking morons," she says. "QC heard there was an accident and he's sniffing all around the plant."

She's wading through a pile of fish, kicking them back into the sand. "Make it look like it just happened. He's on his way down here right now!"

I tell them I'll handle it, strip off my raingear, and sprint over the dunes to the processor.

I catch the QC guy outside the holding tank just as he's starting down to the boatyard. He's got a little flashlight and a digital camera. He's still wearing that stupid white smock like he tests Jell-O in a lab. He stays at a B&B in Paulson and drives a rental to the processor every day.

"Hey," I say to him. "Did you hear about the hose?"

"Yes," he says. "I'm headed down there now to check in on things."

"Great. Where's your gun?"

He just looks at me.

"Flares?"

Nothing.

"You didn't hear? A bear chewed a hole in the line. Then when they pressurized the line, it blew. There's a few bears down there now. A sow with some cubs and at least one male."

He's looking around now, checking over his shoulder. He asks if Helen or Kevin are down there. I tell him I fucking hope not because I don't know who'll run the place without them. He says he really thinks he should check on things down there and I tell him to go right ahead. He looks back at the tank. It's running low. We'll be out of fish before the next tender pulls in.

"A bear's sense of smell is something like seven times better than a bloodhound."

"I just got a call," he says. "I was in bed and the phone rang. A woman said a hose blew and you were running old fish from the beach. Then she hung up."

"Well," I say. "The first half of that's true. Go down and look if you want to."

"How do you plan to pick them up?"

I look at him like he's stupid. I say, "We're not. The bears are."

When he's safely back in the plant, I sprint back down to the beach and tell Helen to radio Ernesto with the bear story. She starts laughing. "That's the dumbest thing I've ever heard."

"Smartest you mean?"

We're almost done by the time a second truck comes down. It runs over a few salmon that go splat under the tires. One of them shoots a string of roe into the brake light. The truck stops, still idling, and a man's voice says, "How goes it, boys?" It's him.

Kevin Haverberger. I can tell by his acorn-shaped head. He slips out of the truck and approaches. "Which one of you is the Beaver?"

I tell him my name's Garrett Deaver but he can call me Beaver because I am an industrious motherfucker.

He picks up a fish, looks it over, and heaves it over the quay onto the mud flats. "Believe it or not," he says, "this is not the first time this has happened. Eleven years ago, the fuckers on strike did the exact same thing. It knocked one of the dock crew ten feet into the air. What can I say? You can't idiot-proof the world."

He starts working alongside us, groaning.

"This," he says, slapping two tails together. "This is getting sent to the dogfood plant probably, but we'll see what we can save from it first. Most years I wouldn't bother, but it's been a shit year so far."

I say, "I thought we were breaking processing records."

"Yeah, for a week we were. Now Fish and Game's getting fussy about the escapement numbers. But I don't know. Salmon operate on their own schedules." He tosses another fish. "So the bears was your idea?"

I say yes and I feel my star start to rise.

"Now I got to go and turn your lie into the truth. It's a good thing they sent Mr. Magoo over here to inspect the plant or I'd have some explaining to do."

"Sorry," I tell him.

"Oh, fuck them. These people. They want wild fish, but they want it perfect. I say, *how much are you willing to pay then?*

And people act like I'm the bad guy. We got mining companies trying to turn Alaska into Swiss cheese, and I run around the state fighting them, losing money, and I get back here and people tell me I'm the bad guy. People write me little petitions. People steal my fish. They mess with my equipment. Tell me I got to do more for the local community."

Bonnie with the pipe wrench over her shoulder. Or was it Bayram's guys?

Kevin says bye and walks to the truck and gets in and puts it into drive. The mounds of fish glowing red in the brake lights like campfires. Then he motions me to the truck. What would it get me if I told him that I saw Bonnie that night? What will it cost me if I don't? I'm thinking through it but he speaks first. "I'm confused about you," he says. "Helen's been singing your praises, saying you ought to be next in line for her job. But then this fucking *strongly worded letter* about wages and timesheets shows up on my desk, and it says Garrett Deaver right there at the top, before all the foreign kids who will be gone in a few days anyway."

"What," I say. "That's not right."

"You're telling me you didn't put your name on anything like that."

"No way," I tell him. "Swear to God."

"I believe it," he says. "These guys, they'll stoop as low as you let him."

He pulls out his black leather wallet and gives me four fifty-dollar bills. "For your work, and for your discretion. We're about to have a slow day tomorrow. You go have a good time."

I say, "Wait," just as he's easing off the brake. "I bet they wrote Bayram's name on there, too. Bayram Demir. Great kid. Those guys have been egging him to sign, but he wouldn't do it."

"Bayram Demir," he says. "Well, we'll see."

When I get back, Bayram and Sven are standing on the quay wall seeing who can throw fish the farthest. Sven throws them overhand, like an axe. Bay goes for more of a hammer throw, spinning a few times and letting one go into the darkness. They can't see where they land so they're trying to settle it by sound. They look like little kids to me.

"Bayram!" I say. "Did you put my fucking name on one of those bullshit petitions of yours?" Even in the half-dark I can see the surprise on his face, and I know he did.

He says, "You said I could. Is that not what you said?"

"We both know I didn't fucking say that."

"My mistake," he says, his voice ticking up at the end.

I turn to leave, stop, change my mind. I take the two-hundred bucks and stick it in his chest. "Take this and stop bitching about your money."

That night, in my bunk, I realize what Kevin said: *gone in a few days anyway.*

The Klak Fancy Letter
Monday, July 17th

Listen Up!

A number of so-called petitions have made their way to my desk in the last week. Klak Fancy prides itself on offering better bonuses and accommodations than any other processor. If you worked anywhere else, you'd be eating beans out of a can and sharing your bunk with rats.

If anyone believes they are subject to workplace discrimination, they are welcome to contact the Alaska Labor Relations Agency. Otherwise, put on your big boy pants and do the job you signed up to do!

While no more salmon have been found chewed on, please keep a look-out for suspicious behavior. Any effort to disrupt the critical work of our processor will be met with termination and **immediate** legal action.

Fish Count: 84,290 (Gotta pick up the pace, Klakers)

Weather: High of 63, light rain. Sunrise—5:45 a.m. Sunset—11:18 p.m.

Alaska Word of the Day: Work—We all know what it means, but not all of us know how to do it! Take pride in what you do every day!

Twenty-Eight

Low fish numbers. At first it feels like that same preseason twitch. Restless dudes tossing rocks at old barrels. Circles of smokers huddled up, whispering. Shift friendships die fast. Back to Turks with Turks, Colombians with Colombians. Some guys don't care about the money anymore. They just want to go home. They want burgers. They want new socks. They're desperate to get laid. And everyone wants someone to blame. Somebody wrote KLAK IS WHACK in chalk on the tin side of the shower house. In the shitter, WE SAY MORE PAY and below that FUCK TURKS and below that FUCK KEVIN and, below that, just FUCK. Last night Jarrod got drunk and ripped the payphones off the wall outside of the bunkhouse. I saw him doing it, too. Bayram and I were standing on the chow house steps, smoking, talking about his troubles with his Turkish friends when Jarrod came limping by. He stopped, grabbed one dirty yellow phone from where it hung on the outer wall, under a little plywood roof that hardly stopped the rain, and he pulled the phone from the cord. He turned around, looked at us, said,

Whoops, and did the same thing to the other two. He put the last one in his hoodie pocket when he walked away.

"Great," Bayram yelled to him. "Now nobody can call their families."

He turned and pitched the phone at us and it smashed against the chow house wall.

When I walked by in the morning, the cords were dangling from the bunkhouse wall like the garter snakes we used to catch as kids. Nick Destin liked to nail them by the head to the rail of his dad's porch.

We get ten hours of work that could be done in eight. Slime line kids keep sneaking over to packing to peek in the freezers and see what's left. Helen tells me not to show them because if I do, they'll slow down even more. I see a Colombian kid looking at my logbooks then whispering to his buddies in packing to chill. I don't even think they'd have to whisper. It's like everyone agreed without talking. The vibe is a sludge, slowing the processor's heart. Guys are going home broke. They know it. And me? There's only maybe seven months before I can come back for herring season. That's not so long. There's fall work in Alaska, helping out with moose hunting camps. That or processing on the Aleutians or a big floating processor in the Bering Sea. Everybody I talk to tells me something different. Crab processing is fine. It's garbage. Cod is good work. It's hell. If only time would either slow down or speed up. Like a toilet or a whirlpool, faster in the middle, up, up, up, and in the dead center a fish's eye, blinking back at me again. It knows. I take a yaba from my freezer suit, swallow it with spit.

"Hey!" Bayram's walking across the packing floor in his street clothes, that same hoodie that says OH YEAH! We're on different shifts now that the fishing's slow.

He says, "Did you know? What did you even know?"

"You're not supposed to be in here without raingear."

"My friends were just sent home," he says. "Sent home without bonuses. Charged room and board. It was everyone who helped gather signatures for the petitions. Everyone but me."

"I told you I would look out for you."

"Don't you get it?" he says. "They're going to think it was me! They were all planning to walk out during the next run of salmon and stand in the breakroom until they could negotiate. They are going to think I betrayed them."

I say, "There is no next big run."

"That is not the point," he says. But his face drops like it is the point. "I go to university with those guys. Some of them know my family. They're going to talk about all of this at home. They are going to tell everyone I manipulated them. I won't even be back to defend myself. I have got to get to Klak and email my sisters before they hear any of this."

He can't even look at me. His face turned down to the concrete.

He says, "I am still waiting on my iPods or else I would just go."

"Hey," I say. "At least you got to see that bear, right?"

He says, "You know that no one likes you. No one believes a single word you say."

Twenty-Nine

I look for him on break and again when shift ends. I look even though I don't know what to say. I *was* thinking about him. I *was* trying to help. I'm not like my dad. Two hours of searching, and when I tell Sven about it, he says maybe Bayram went to High-liners, the other bar in Klak. He says let's go.

It's classier than the Black Dog. There's paint on the walls. The barstools still have some stuffing and nobody's allowed to smoke inside. If the fishermen are bummed about the slow fishing, they don't show it. I take a yaba, then another. I ask Sven why he thought Bayram would be here and he laughs at me. He says he could tell I just needed to chill. He says we'll find Bayram later. Here's a beer. Here's a shot. Here are some of Ernesto's cousins.

"Hey. Tell 'em about that leg bone."

So I do. There were toes on it. Skin, sinew. They love it. They love the knowledge I have to give them. They have all sorts of theories. Someone killed over meth. No, suicide. No, an accident way upriver. Somebody from a tourist lodge in the mountains. The hot wife of a media mogul. The man from the bear house. We laugh and talk shit and things get light and loose. Sven is reassuring. Bayram will be fine! Bayram's scrappy. Bayram's a winner. Bayram's up two-hundred bucks, money *you* gave him, Beaver—money *you* gave *him*.

Now, a pair of small hands circle my face and cup my eyes. They're cool and rough and it's dark. Bonnie?

"Guess."

"Kevin Haverberger."

"Nope."

"Hillary Clinton."

"I don't know if that's hotter or colder."

"It's somebody with fishy hands," I say.

Helen's with Heather, who works in the office. I've never seen Helen's hair, had no idea it was red. "Come," she says. "Both of you."

We follow them to one corner of the bar with the window facing the bay. The bay's rough. The waves are white, like Pennsylvania hills in the winter. Helen says she's avoiding somebody and it's up to Sven and me to keep them entertained. I say sure thing, boss. I tell her I can walk on my hands and she laughs like I'm kidding.

Heather says, "Who has gossip on the hose?"

I say, "Maybe it was just an accident."

"Do you know how unlikely that is?" Heather says. "I'm telling you. I saw Kevin right when he got the call. He was freaked. Especially after the electric thing. All he cared about was making sure the QC guy didn't get wind of it."

Sven says, "I got money on the net lady. The other night she came down into the roe house and completely lost her shit because somebody parked her in. We would've just moved the truck but she went nuts, man. She slammed the door so hard the glass broke."

"I don't know," I say. "She's harmless."

"Everybody has some sort of problem with Kevin."

Helen pokes me in the chest. "His nephew took Beaver's job. Maybe it was him."

"Yeah," I say. "And I pounded a nail in Jarrod's foot, too."

Everybody laughs.

Sven says, "And I'm eating the salmon!"

"That's gotta be Ernesto," Heather says. "That dude's got at least one weird joke every year. A few years ago they had to shoot a nuisance bear after it kept hanging around the chow house and Ernesto cut its head off with a power saw and kept hiding it at different spots in the maintenance building. Under wheelbarrows and shit."

Sven brings us another round.

Helen says, "Everyone talks shit about Kevin but without him, half the stuff in this town wouldn't be here."

"Isn't that the problem, though? Pretty soon he'll have the dog food factory. He's hellbent on getting all that unused land around the processor to expand," Sven says.

"Like that old house?" I say, and all at once it makes sense. Bonnie.

"He's a small fry," Heather says. "Neptune's twenty times worse than this place. And in the grand scheme of things, Pebble Mine's a hundred times worse than them."

"Here's to fish," Heather says.

Blub—downed.

Sven says, "You wanna peace?" and Heather stands, takes her coat.

"Are they . . . ?"

"Knowing Sven," Helen says. "Yep."

Quiet.

"Well," she tells me. "I think you're in line for a supervisor job coming up."

"What! When?"

"Next spring if you want it," she says. "You gotta promise to keep it quiet."

She sticks out her pinky, and I stick out mine, and they thread together, and she's leaning in close. "Kevin heard they're going to do a temporary closure of the fishery. Just two days, while the state can figure out how to set the escapement. So we're going to have to thin the herd."

"Are you the one doing the thinning?"

"Not by myself. But yeah, some of it."

"Can you keep Bayram? Turkish guy on the slime line. He's a great worker."

I look down. Our pinkies are still interlocked. Her hand's tiny. Then it's gone. Then it's on her beer.

"Yeah," she says. "I can try."

"I can vouch for him."

More beers and blurry eyes and we end up swapping bios. She's from Portland, before it started getting hip. Her parents are high-school teachers, *her* high-school teachers, which is why she never liked school.

"I came to Alaska first for a summer outdoor program," she says. "We walked on glaciers and all that bullshit. We had to feed sled dogs, then one of them bit a girl's ear off and she went home. It was a program *just* for young women. Wild Women of Alaska. But there was just something about it. We had this circle of truth every night. And that shit was *mandatory*. Girls talked about being assaulted, girls coming out. I don't know. I just felt like nothing bad enough ever happened to me to be included, you know? Am I talking a lot?"

"Nope!"

"None of that outdoor job stuff ever materialized, and I ended up here. It was right after the whole program, and salmon was starting, and I just didn't have any time for any more feelings. I just kicked the fucking door down."

"I get it," I tell her.

"No, you don't."

"You're right. I don't. But parts of it, I get."

Now she's rolling her eyes at me. "The thing about you, Garrett, is that it's hard to ever get a sense of what you're really thinking. You got this little shitty grin all the time. But then you act so goddamn sincere."

I think about those headlines Mr. Pritchard used to read to me.

She says, "There you go. That little side smile. How did you end up here?"

I say, "It was an accident, more or less."

"Well, which is it? More or less?"

Thirty

The sun flickers and dies and the sky looks like an old TV powering down. Helen's shack has one porthole window on the plywood door. One wall's painted pale pink, the rest raw plywood spotted with pine knots. She clicks on a reading lamp next to the cot and unscrews the naked overhead bulb with her bare hand. Her shadow's huge on the wall. Her clothes are laying all around the floor. Her boots are coming off, and she says, "There's no way in hell I'm sucking your dick, so don't bother asking."

She says, "Fuck, we stink," as we peel off each other's layers, each one with its own special smell, down to the pale skin. I see myself in the warped mirror on the wall and realize she's seeing more of me than I've seen of me in a month. I'm skinnier now, carved with new muscles. New lines, new shadows. Is this how other people see me? No, Garrett, focus—her hands, her mouth, the way our teeth click together, her tattoos, pink flowers and vines along her shoulders and chest. I trace them with my lips and feel something like fear, fear and maybe awe. Like the first time the freezer door closed on me and I was all along in the swirl. That's it. Swirling.

Her skin's soft and the shack's cold. Her hands are cold and her hips feel cold and I try not to squirm as she rubs her cold hands down my back. But the warmth comes, friction, sweat, and when we fuck each other, our smells fuck each other too. They rise above us and mix into one smell, our smell, a bad smell all at once smelling good. I lift my head to breathe it in and one of those pine knots winks at me.

"What's wrong?"

I say, "Tell me what you like, tell me what you want, tell me what to do to you," because I've learned that people like to be asked about themselves.

She says, "Why do I always have to be in charge?"

And after we're done, nested on the cot, I can't stop wondering if that meant she trusted me to do a good job.

Thirty-One

"Hey, you gotta go."

Gray dawn out the porthole and the lamp flashes on. The alarm clock says 4:35 a.m. She lays there quiet while I look around for my clothes. I'm missing a sock. I'm missing a T-shirt. I want to stay longer.

"Thanks," she says when I sit down at the edge of the bed to put my boots on. "I must've needed that." I reach under the blanket, into the warmth, and I rub her calf, the velvety hairs, and I'm desperate to stay, to get lost in this place, but then her skin is gone, and its cold, and she's saying, "Don't. I'm ticklish." I say sorry to the touching. You're welcome for the sex.

I'm half out the door before she says, "I almost forgot! I asked Kevin about Pennsylvania Joe for you, and he said he didn't remember anything. What's up?"

I'd forgot I asked her at all. It was during that big run of fish. I tell her I just saw a picture of this guy on the wall of the Black Dog, somebody I maybe knew.

She says, "Wasn't there anything in the scrapbook?"

WHAT—

"It's actually pretty cool. The woman who runs the place keeps this book behind the bar that goes with all the photos. Just names and dates, newspaper clippings, shit like that. People are always looking at it in there."

"I had no idea."

"There's pictures of Kevin in there when he had hair."

I say Thanks, thanks for fucking me and being fucked by me, and I walk out into the gray morning, the sky swirled like a pearl, and I take the long way back to the bunkhouse, past the empty chow house, and the dumpster with the birds fighting for spots along the rail. Do they know nobody's inside cooking? First time in a month I've seen the kitchen lights off. Overhead a raven squawks and it sounds so much like the word *Hey* I turn around and my heart explodes because I think maybe it's Helen, telling me to come back and stay a little longer.

In the bunkhouse the workers sleep sad and unfucked with T-shirts draped over the faces to keep out the light and their ugly feet sticking out from the ends of their cots. It looks like a mortuary and smells just a little better. There's practically name tags on their toes. A sad row of suckers, funeral quiet, too tired to know anything. What do they even know? What do they even dream? I can't remember the last dream I had. It's been weeks. I think about the way that Sven just floats through life, half asleep, and I can't help but feel jealous. I was always the kind of kid who fought sleep, who refused to accept inevitability. I'd prop myself half off the bed so that when my head drooped I'd wake and go back to the TV. My dad was the same way. You'd catch him up at two, three in the morning. He smoked Black & Mild cigars, wine flavored, two for a dollar, smoke so thick you could eat it. I'd see him from my bedroom window, leaning against his truck, his redneck friends long gone, the cigar's red cherry in the dark like a Cyclops eye.

It was a Wednesday when my mom called with the news. The first nice day of the year, and I was looking out my dorm window at all the muddy grass watching students hunt out the driest patches to put blankets. She didn't even ask if I was sitting down. She said, "Your father, Duane, has passed away. He fell from a balcony in Hawaii. He had been living in Alaska."

I remember looking down from the window and asking myself if anything had gone through his head on the way down. Was the balcony high enough for regrets? Could he even remember my face?

What's the last thing to go through a bug's mind when he hits the windshield?

His ass!

He used to tell that joke all the time.

His ass—

    His ass—

        His ass—

The Klak Fancy Letter
Tuesday, July 18th

Hello Klakers,

Tonight at midnight, the Alaska Department of Fish and Game will issue a temporary closure of the majority of the sockeye fishing districts in Bristol Bay. That means we will be out of fish for a day or two. This happens occasionally when the numbers of fish don't match the preseason forecasts.

Schedule:

*Shift A: Report to the processor at your usual time.

* Shift B: Report to your supervisor in the mess hall at 9:00 a.m. Do **not** clock in before reporting.

*Shift C: Report to your supervisor at the processor at 2:00 p.m. Do **not** clock in before reporting.

Important Updates:

*Report suspicious behavior!!!!

*Laundry Service is suspended during the closure. So are all break room snacks and beverages.

Weather: High of 63, light rain. Sunrise—5:47 a.m. Sunset—11:16 p.m.

Alaska Word of the Day: Fisheries Management—Fisheries management is the practice of controlling the number of fish that can be caught and processed by hard-working workers like you! The State of Alaska **strictly** controls the number of fish that can be caught commercially.

Thirty-Two

7 a.m. No sleep since I left Helen's shack. I laid there thinking about death and then about money, thinking up ways to help Bayram. I'm going to give him my hours if Helen and Ernesto let me. That's all I can think to do.

The whole crew slugs inside the break room for work instructions. They look like they're rotting. Missing gloves, stained and stinking, yellow eyes, leaning against the tables, holding their foreheads, gulping at water and coffee and arguing about who puked where last night. One of the Ukrainian kids has a split lip. One of the Moldovan kids has his shirt on inside out. One of the Americans smells like sex and that person is me. Helen looks hungover, too. She's wearing a bandana over her throat to cover the hickey I gave her. She told me not to tell anybody, and I won't. But I wish she'd never told me about the scrapbook at the bar. Because it's obvious, ain't it? I'm going to the Black Dog tonight. Even if Helen said meet me in my shack. Even if Kevin said you're a supervisor, starting now, I'd still be at the Black Dog. That shit's foregone, man. Magnetite—

... His ass.

    ... His ass.

        ... His ass.

Helen sticks two pinkies between her lips and whistles so loud a kid drops his coffee cup.

She says, "Glad I got your attention. We still have several fucktons of work to do, so I'm going to keep it short. The deal's that Fish and Game has decided to shut down fishing for a day or two. Just while they try to figure out what's going on. That's obviously not good news. We still have work for everyone. But first. I know things got a little wild last night."

All the workers laugh. Bayram walks in late, sits down on the bench in front of me.

She says, "You all have got to act like adults around here. You break rules, you do some dumb shit, you get fired. The season isn't over, and we'll need everybody to kick it back into high gear when the fish come flooding in. Because they will. They always do. We're going to give everyone eight hours today and six tomorrow." Noise rises up, like a bunch of bugs. HARD WORKER complains that this isn't fair.

She says, "You take your hours or you take your bullshit back to Anchorage."

He stands up and says they want twelve hours. His girlfriend is up now, too, and two Colombian guys next to her. Bayram tries to stand and I put my hand on his shoulder and push him back down. Helen says there's nothing to talk about it. She just keeps repeating it—nothing, nothing, nothing to talk about—and all at once the Colombians are out the door.

"There you go," she says. "More work for the rest of you."

She tells me to take a crew to the boneyard and I do, the whole troupe following me through the processor grounds. I might as well be playing the flute. It's warm, a bluebird sky, and the sun's so bright it boils some water out of my eyes.

"It's nice out," I say.

Bayram doesn't look at me. He just walks past. I hurry and catch him and say Helen's right. More fish are coming. We just got to hang tight.

"That's not what you said yesterday," he says.

"I was wrong. Want more hours? You can have mine."

He's stopped now, standing at the top of the dune with his head like a tiny cloud blocking out the sun. He says, "You think I'm some sort of project? Something to make you feel better?"

But that's not it, and I say so. I say he's my friend, my buddy, and I haven't made many friends, here or any place else, and people have a tendency to dislike me, and I want to help him help his family, maybe out of guilt, so what, so what I want somebody to think I'm decent, but more than that, way more than that, I want to be *able* to help, to have something worth offering, and this is what I got, some hours, and yeah that makes me feel better, and so what, am I not allowed to feel better? Am I just supposed to feel bad?

I'm not even done explaining and I can see his face change. He's squinting, even with the sun at his back. I know that look. It's Pritchard. It's Helen early this morning and Nick Destin and trailer park Randy making a show out of giving me that bike. But mostly it's my mom, my mom on her knees scrubbing blood, shaking her head. Her pity, and the push/pull response that pity brings. Those SPCA ads with little dogs like flea-market foot stools. Nasty cats with one bulging eye, and you love them *because* they're pathetic. You stare because you want to look away. That's pity, love with disgust on the edges. Bayram says it without saying it. He says it with his face.

"Besides," I say, shrugging, "I'm just ready for some down time, you know?"

Thirty-Three

In the boneyard, sparks fly. Two maintenance guys are cutting up an old steel tugboat with acetylene torches and a teardrop-shaped blob of molten metal stretches and drops sizzling into the sand. At the maintenance garage Ernesto's smoking and drinking from a two-liter bottle of Pepsi. Next to him is the old guy that we saw walk past the bear one night.

"Beaver," Ernesto says. "And goons!" He doles out sledge-hammers and crowbars and hacksaws from a pile he'd made near the door to the maintenance building. Two Polish kids just get pieces of metal pipe. One kid gets an axe. Two just get gloves. "You can move the scraps," he tells them.

"Listen," he says. "When things get slow, work goes to the best workers. And you know who makes that decision?"

Bayram says, "Beaver thinks he does."

"Maybe soon," Ernesto says. "Come, goons. I'll get you started."

There's a skiff, a dory, and a gillnetter all lined up smallest to biggest in the sand above the tide line. Dad, mom, baby—like coffins of a nice family popping up after a flood. Ernesto says they've been out of commission for years and no one has made the time to tear them apart. Until now. He says to break them down and stack the wood. He says it's very simple. Even goons can do it. What are you waiting for? Isn't work what you wanted?

"Beaver," he says, "Come and have a break with us. You look like dog shit."

We stand under the open bay door and watch the crew work. Hammers swinging, the squawk of pulled nails, arguments over how to proceed. I love the animal way that work happens. How the crew just falls together into a plan. They hardly even know it's happening. But it is. Even the hammers fall into a natural rhythm.

Ernesto says, "My cousin told me he saw you at Highliners last night. Told me about that bone you found." He elbows the old guy next to him. "I was just telling you about that."

"That right there was that man's boat." He points. "At least I think so."

I ask if he's shitting me.

"I'd put money on it."

"You're shitting me."

(There's an awful lot of yaba shooting lasers in my head right now.)

"You didn't hear this from me," the old guy says. His voice is low and dusty. "But it was maybe old Otis whose leg you found. He's the only person to really go missing here in the last few years. As in *missing* missing."

"This was before your time," Ernesto says.

"Let me tell it," the guy says. "You're terrible at stories."

He says, "Otis was the net lady's man. He was a real asshole. Made her look like the normal one. Those two were always just bitching at each other. Every time you saw them they were having it out about something. But a few years ago, they got into it one day in the parking lot of the Black Dog so bad that the cops had to come. Supposedly it was about that boat right there. Otis wanted to fix it up and run a set net. She wouldn't give him the money to do it."

"No, that's not right," Ernesto interjects. "She wanted to fix it up. She was attached to it. What's the word? Sentimental. But he wouldn't have anything to do with it."

"Doesn't matter," the old man says. "The point is they had a hell of a row about it. I believe he laid his hands on her. She actually pulled a gun out her truck and waved it around. And he was saying, *Just fucking shoot me, then.* The cop came and put her in cuffs and everything. I was there, at the bar. I thought somebody might get shot."

"Hey you know what?" Ernesto says. "You're a friend of hers, Beaver. I'm not sure you need to be hearing all of this."

I watch him turn his head and look down at the crew. They've ripped the planks off half of the skiff and with the long black ribs exposed it looks like something stripped clean of its meat. "No," I say. "I think I do."

They look at each other. The old man's smoking again.

"Fuck it," he says. "The real gist of it is that they had that huge falling out, the fight of a lifetime, a fight when she *threatens* to shoot him. And a couple of days later, the fucker's gone. They said he likely drowned, probably suicide, but everyone knows she's crazy."

It's not like I'm some sort of bone expert, she'd told me, with a shack full of bones.

Ernesto says, "It gets worse, my man. I saw Otis the day before he went missing. Maybe I was the last person to even see that fucker alive. And when I saw him, we bullshitted for a bit and it seemed mostly normal. But you know what he said to me that really fucked me up?"

"What?" I say. "What did he say?"

"He told me not to say."

"What?"

"I shouldn't."

"WHAT?"

Ernesto takes a step toward me, leans in close, and lets loose a trumpetous fart.

He says, "Gotcha Motherfucker!"

The two of them throw their heads back laughing. They're still laughing when I walk away. Even after the sound dies I can feel the H's and A's following me down to the quay. There's a full army of them. They're marching in formation across the sand. I know if I run, they'll chase me. They always do.

Thirty-Four

I'm standing on the dunes below the Black Dog with the scrapbook of wrecked boats unopened in my hands. Fishermen keep stumbling around the corner, unzipping, and saying "My Bad" when they see me on the hill. One guy almost pissed on my head. I tell myself this is why I haven't opened it. I just need the right place. The right private second. But come on, Garrett. We both see what's going on here. I thought the scrapbook would be red but it's not. It's the same gray as the sea. Mental illness gray. There's a comic strip glued to the front with Ahab in a top hat, looking down at a cute little whale.

The caption says, *I swear it was bigger in my mind.*

It's clear out. Clear and warm. People are saying the shit fishing might have something to do with the rain. That or the heat. Or the bad floods a few years back. Nobody knows anything, especially me. I really do hope it was the guilt. That he jumped as an apology. I know how that sounds, but it's true.

Earlier, I'd heard that everyone was going to the Black Dog and I figured it'd be crowded. I've been growing a beard and I kept my hood up. The whole place reeked of smoke and processing. At the pool table, a few fishermen shot pool for fifty bucks a ball even though the big sign above the tables read "No Guns, No Gambling, No Politics." There was one TV in the corner. An explosion in the Sunni Triangle.

I sifted through the foremen and fishermen, careful not to bump their beers, and at the end of the bar I saw the old drunk who maybe tried to shoot me. At the other end of the bar, a young Native woman was pouring beers for a bunch of grinning white guys in matching Neptune fleeces. They looked clean and wore big satellite phones on their belts. When they lined up against the wall for a photo, I did a funny trick—I lifted one of their beers and walked away. There was an empty space on the wall where my father's picture was and at first my mind went conspiratorial. Then I remembered how the frame had smashed. I thought about that thing that Flex had told me about the femurs. Burst fractures. I could taste the roar of the room, the eye-level smoke. It would be really nice to pull some racks of fish.

Someone clapped me on my back and spilled some of my beer.

"Beaver, you're slopping all over yourself." It was Sven. He was so high it looked like you could blindfold him with a piece of string. He said he was stoked to get a little R&R to get his mind right, get his mind right, get his mind right.

Get his mind right. But Sven was on my left.

"You looking for someone?" he asked me.

"No."

He dribbled some liquor from a flask into my glass.

"Boilermaker," he said. "Desperate times and all that."

I could have just asked him to go get me the scrapbook. But he'd need to know why. He always needed to know why. It was him who'd put the bone in my mind after all, who made me get drunk and tell Ernesto's cousins. Was it all one big joke he pulled on me? We drank and repeated and soon my eyes retreated further back in my head and all the hard edges got hammered soft. It was hot in the bar, pinheads of sweat. The hum of people living. Everyone in there had a life far from Klak, but it was hard to remember being anywhere else. I tried to remember faces I knew from before. My mom's, Pritchard's, Nick Destin's. None of them came.

Repeat.

In the corner of the bar, in front of the dirty window overlooking the bay, the backlit silhouette of Bonnie caught my eye. Her tiny frame, her nest of curls. She had a bottle of beer in her hand, and she was waving it while she talked to Ernesto. She shook her head, and he shook his head again. Everyone in the bar simultaneously shook their head. Then, all at once, like they were connected to the same string, and the string was pulled by someone up above, they both turned and looked at me and turned back to one another and kept on arguing.

I wasn't feeling so great.

Then, in the parking lot, Sven and I ran into a couple forklift drivers from Neptune, crust punk types with stick-and-poke tattoos and haircuts like they'd lost some sort of bet. Sven and one of them went around the side of the building to smoke and left us standing there. I told him I had a quick job for him.

I said it'd take ten minutes and he'd get fifty bucks. When he came back, the scrapbook was stuffed under his hoodie. "Just take the fucking thing back when you're done," he said. "That lady doesn't take a lot of shit."

Now, when I start flipping, I see his face in every photo. Even in the grainy black-and-whites of Filipino fishermen on their tiny sailboats. Even when they're smiling, they look so hard. They look like soldiers. Maybe that's it, the pride. I'd hated him for being gone, but somehow his stories always managed to turn the anger into pride. All that shit I told my friends about his job—did I say it until I believed it?

Then, the real him. There in the middle. We must look a lot alike now, me in my beard and windburned cheeks. He's standing on the shore on a rock the size of a tipped-over pop machine with his hands interlocked on the top of his head. He's soaking wet and he looks like hell. Behind him, there's a little bowpicker busted up on a rock, maybe fifty feet from the shore.

It reads: *Joel Shultz with the F/V Steadfast, grounded near Ekuk. 1994 or 5.*

Thirty-Five

Bonnie's not in the bar, so I leave the book on an empty stool and jet before the bartender can see me. It's still light outside, maybe 10 p.m. I didn't steal the picture. I don't need it. I wear his face just underneath my own. The parking lot's full of trucks and I'm remembering the wet cry of his windshield wipers. I was little. It was early and raining and he'd scooped me from my bed and carried me to the truck and I didn't even think to ask why. My shoes were in the truck already, along with some of my clothes and a cooler. He had a coffee in one cup holder and a beer in the other. He'd been up all night drinking with his buddies and now he was patting my head. He got that way sometimes after he was out late. Tender. Sappy, even. Some mornings I'd wake up and find him cocooned around me in my tiny bed, still in his boots and jacket. Other times he'd wake me up to talk. Just to tell me stories. I'd forgotten all about that until right now. Is that what my mom meant when she said there were signs he'd kill himself? Maybe I just mistook that for love.

In the truck, he said, "sleep" and I did, thinking, maybe, maybe, Alaska—

The bump of a gravel road woke me up. It was light, barely. Wooly gray. Talk radio. He liked Rush Limbaugh. He was smoking a cigar, leaning out the window to keep the smoke from the cab. My mouth tasted sour. I asked where we were and he said, "The woods."

I drifted again and by the time we pulled off the road, it was morning. Moving water, I could hear it through the trees. He had fishing poles in the back and he led me down some path lined with Busch cans to a crick lined with pines. He hadn't thought to bring any bait so he showed me how to pull apart a rotten log and find grubs. He smoked and drank his coffee and gave me some string cheese and a warm Mountain Dew. We didn't catch anything or say anything or really even do anything, but I didn't care.

Was that fishing to him? Was it life?

I start down the road to Klak and make it almost halfway when Bonnie speeds by me and brakes and the transmission whines in reverse back down the road, swerving. She rolls down the passenger window and holds the door shut when I try to open it. "You fucking dummy," she says. "I can't believe you went back to the bar."

"Can I get a ride?"

"No, I'm drunk."

I jerk open the door and get in anyway.

I ask if she's actually drunk and she guns it, grinding through gears on the flat road. She's driving fast, too fast. Some bebop stuff is playing on the radio. The window's down, dust storming through the car. I tell her I need to talk to her, and she says after this next song. We see the cannery, zip past it. From there the road cuts straight like an incision through the taiga. We pass the mounded landfill—eagles, ravens, gulls, bulldozer—and the swampland with the black trees tilted like drunks. We pass the cabins along the river with their roofs sprouting old satellite dishes. It's windy. A piece of cardboard cartwheels across the road and down a driveway, where it's attacked by a fat sled dog on a chain. I think, man, that dog has really let himself go. I think about yelling stop. Jumping out. Unhooking that dog and making for the mountains. Like in those old Jack London books. Nobody goes to a fish processor to find themselves. I've been doing it wrong this whole time!

Before I can ask her about Joel Shultz, she says, "Kevin's really trying to put the screws to me, Garrett. Ernesto just let it slip that they're gonna tear down my shack. I built that shack. It's more like home than my house. But fuck them. And fuck you, while we're at it. What were you doing back there at the Black Dog?"

I say, "Joel Shultz."

She just looks at me. She looks for way too long. The car drifts a little. Now we're taking our half out of the middle and Bonnie's still looking at me or maybe past me. I reach for the wheel and she slaps my hand.

"Please slow down."

"We're here."

Paulson. A grocery store, hardware store, a few restaurants, a school under renovation with singlewide trailers serving as classrooms. At the edge of town, a tourist lodge that's so shiny it looks like it's been polished with spit. Past that the low hills become mountains in the haze. Somewhere there's a forest fire burning. You can see the smoke haze swirling in the sky, smell it overtop the dust.

"Joel Shultz. Did you know him?"

"Barratry," she says, turning around in the dirt lot of the lodge. "It's when you scuttle a boat for an insurance payout."

The deer in the truck bed.

"That's him," I say. "His name's Duane."

We're headed back through town.

"I thought you had to go to Paulson."

"I changed my mind. So was that your dad, Joel Shultz?"

"Duane Deaver."

"I did a couple nets for him. I think he deckhanded for a while, then went in on a boat with Weird Steve Peterson, the guy that owns *The Matthew*."

I'd worked with Steve in the beginning of the year. He was one of my steady boatyard gigs, the reason I met Bonnie at all. It'd been right there and I didn't even know what I should've been asking.

"Your dad and Steve and about twenty of those bible thumping sons-of-bitches didn't strike. They didn't even let it be known that they weren't going to strike. They just slipped out there and all got to be highliners for a week or two. I thought Otis was going to kill one of them. He did slash some tires. I think someone's dog got poisoned. Otis said he'd never do that, but I don't know. They sabotaged some boats."

"Like my dad's?"

"Oh fuck no. He did that himself. Those guys made their money. But we made it hell for them after. I figured that's why your dad scuttled his boat. Lots of guys got out after that. Everybody's on the edge of going broke, so anytime something bad happens boats go up for sale like you wouldn't believe."

A fox shoots across the road and Bonnie brakes so hard my head hits the dash.

"Sorry," she says. "They're my favorite."

"My dad died," I say. "I told you already. About four months ago now. He jumped off a hotel balcony."

She says, "Jesus, Garrett. They're always doing that in the off-season. When Otis went, they told me fishermen and farmers had the highest suicide rates. It's even worse in some of the Native villages. It spreads like a virus."

"You never told me what happened to Otis."

She rolls the windows up. "You're right. I didn't."

We're quiet for a while. Too long, maybe a mile.

"Otis," she says. "I never even say his name out loud anymore. He and Kevin were friends. The three of us were. They fished together for maybe five years together. Kevin wasn't much of a fisherman but he had some seed money. When he started this place, he roped Otis into helping with some of the setup. I'd been mending nets in Homer, and Otis begged me to move out here. He had some problems. But I said fine. Seemed like up here everybody had some sort of problem then. It was back when you could really escape, you know?"

"Anyway," she says, turning off the radio. "Otis was a fisherman through and through, and when the gillnetters wanted to strike, Otis struck. He said it was just business, but Kevin couldn't take it. Even after the strike was over and everything was settled, Kevin just blacklisted him. Tried to get all the other processors to do the same. I wanted to move down to Ketchikan or Sitka and get a little troller. I could make a little art and we could troll and just sort of ease into retirement."

"But Otis wouldn't hear of moving, even after Kevin bought us out of the processor. So Otis sold his boat and got certified to guide hunts. That was about the worst thing for him, mentally. You know what kind of people spend ten, twelve grand to come to Alaska and kill a brown bear? A bunch of suits. A few years of that, and he just went sort of backward. Somewhere in there I left, moved into Klak. I'll handle some bad traits, but self-pity is one thing I can't stand."

I hadn't noticed it, but she'd pulled off the road by the old bear house in the woods and now we're just idling there. "I know I should've done more with the house afterward. But fuck it. I don't ever want to see anything like that ever again. The blood."

She unlocks the doors. "Get. I got somewhere to be."

"Wait," I say. "If you don't want to lose your shack, then why do you keep fucking with the plant?"

"Me? I figured that was those petition kids. If I was gonna do it, I'd do it right."

Thirty-Six

Back at the processor the Moldovans have a driftwood bonfire on the beach because they're all going home in the morning. It's windy and the fire keeps changing directions, the flames darting off like screams in the dark, and the heat's driving the beach fleas from the sand so that nobody'll sit down for fear of getting gnawed on. There's a few cases of Natty Ice in the sand and a battery-powered stereo blaring pop music that sounds like crinkled tinfoil through the overworked speaker. Everybody's side-eyeing me, sketchy, like I'm part of some sort of cannery cabal, like I'm responsible for the shit season and the shit pay and the firings. Am I? A month ago I would've mistaken the way they look at me for respect.

Bayram's here, drunk, teaching some American kids how to dance. He spreads his arms out from his sides and undulates them, like a curtain of northern lights is passing through him. His knees bend so that he bobs up and down. It's the kind of move that uses a backward logic. The more you think about it, the worse you get. He grabs at their hands as he explains, trying to get everyone involved.

"I need to talk to you," I say to him.

"Later," he says. "You don't dance?"

"Never."

"Very boring," he says. "Did you hear the good news?"

It's hard to imagine any, until he tells me that there will be work tomorrow. Boats are headed back out right now. I tell him again I'll get him extra hours, and he leaves me to dance. First, it's mostly just Bayram and the Europeans. But the enthusiasm grows, it's contagious, until even Sven and Smitty start clopping around in their boots, their jeans tucked inside because of the fleas. Everyone's smoking, always smoking, warm beers in their hands, firelight on their faces, smoke in their eyes.

"Bayram!"

He just keeps dancing. I drink and wait. The Moldovans sway arm-and-arm, laughing at two American kids playing a game of Burn, a lit cigarette smoldering in the gap between their touching forearms until one of them caves. I used to play that game a lot with Nick Destin. I could beat anybody at the trailer park, frat houses too, and now I have a dozen cigarette scars on my forearm. They're shiny and puckered. Like a cat's asshole.

"Hey," I say. "The scar will look exactly like a cat's asshole."

They ignore me.

"You'll remember me someday when you look down and see a cat's asshole."

It's as cold as it's been since May. Hoods drawn tight around our faces, spare hands buried in our pockets, we scrounge the beach in turns for scrap wood to burn. Everyone finally passes the point of dancing and turns to lamenting their lost processing money. When the fire gets low, people start to split for the bunkhouses. I finally grab Bayram to talk but HARD WORKER sees us and says, "Tell me honestly. Is it true that we'll get better hours?"

"To be honest," I say. "I don't really know."

Just then the fire rears up. It's Jarrod, kicking the charred ends of driftwood back into the coals. He's got a pallet under each arm. He says there's a couple more behind the bunkhouse.

"Let's get this bitch going," he says. "It's cold as balls."

I watch him take three beers from the Moldovans' case, sock them in his hoodie pockets. He doesn't even try to hide it. He stares right at me, and his face is orange in the fire, then him and a couple processor kids walk up to the bunkhouse to get those pallets. By then the fire's big, almost head-height, throwing the kind of heat back at us that nobody wants to leave. The music starts back up. It's a party again. And when the processor kids come back with another pallet, I notice Jarrod isn't even with them.

That doesn't make any sense.

"Bay," I say. "Help me go get some more wood."

Thirty-Seven

"Those pills are doing something to your mind," Bayram says. "You sound crazy again."

Maybe, sure, but not about this. I try to explain but the words keep stumbling. Not Bonnie, not Bayram—who?

"I don't care," he says. "You were right about just keeping my head down. All I want is to do my work and make my money and collect my iPods. That's it."

"Real quick," I say. "Five minutes, tops."

We walk through the dark from the bunkhouse past Bonnie's shack, where a few drunk cannery kids are rocking the net truck back and forth in the sand like they can flip it on its side.

"You guys seen Jarrod?"

They point off toward the supervisor shacks.

"You shouldn't be doing that," I tell them.

"You shouldn't be doing that," one of them says back in a high girly voice.

As we're walking away I can hear the truck window smash. Laughter and more broken glass. Things are getting weird, or maybe they always were, like there's something toxic in the air and we've finally passed the safe threshold, too many parts per million now, and I grab Bayram by the arm and we keep going, past the shower house where HARD WORKER and his girl-friend are tip-toeing in together, giggling in their ratty towels, and past Helen's shack, where the light's on, and I can hear her talking to someone, saying, "I'll never live this down!"

A man's voice—Sven?—"He said what?!"

Fumbling in the dark, Bayram behind me, stepping on my long trail of nerves, zapping me, tugging at me, whispering to leave it be, whispering let's go back to the fire, and I start to think he's right, this is more of that legbone bullshit, more of the yaba bragging in my heart, but in the alders past Jarrod's shack, a flashlight beam moves through the woods, over the little stream, toward the bear house past it.

"You see that, too?"

He sees it too. Thank fucking God he sees it too.

"It is probably nothing. Probably just some workers."

I tell him I'm going. He tells me he's not. He's going to bed. He thinks I am unwell. He thinks I should sleep. Goodbye, and I walk alone through the alders in the dark, following the over-grown muddy path, the devil's club scratching at me, the mud trying to slurp me up, my heartbeat in my fingertips, and at the little stream, the board overtop it is wet with footprints, and the moon's out now, blurred like a thumbnail dug into your cheek, and I cross the board and climb the little knoll and see it—the A-frame with the buckling porch in the low light. The front door's boarded shut but there's a smashed-out window that leads to the kitchen.

When I step on the porch the boards bow and now it's coming to me that this is the spot of a suicide, the place that sent Bonnie on her path, and that's what brought us together, really, and I might never make it to that sidewalk in Hawaii, but this might feel the same, this might end it, all those intrusive thoughts, and the hurt is leeching out of the boards, and I'm holding onto a casket, deciding whether to open the lid, deciding whether to finally look, and the flash of light from inside the house tells me I got to. I climb through the low broken window into the kitchen. On the counter by the window, a cheese grater, a corkscrew, nests where chipmunks have been. Hard pill-shaped turds everywhere. On the counter next to the sink, dishes in the rack, still waiting to get put away. I see them and my heart breaks for Bonnie and I notice a coffee cup just like the one in her shack and I grab it and I tip-toe to the threshold and peek into the living room, and there's Jarrod, just a silhouette, his broad back to me, and he's got cushions from an old couch in a pile on the floor, and he's chugging one of those stolen beers. I can hear it draining down his throat. A shadow cuts the light coming in from the window, a second of darkness, and he startles and turns and says, "Uncle?"

The flashlight flicks on, focuses on me. When I look down I see the gas can at his feet.

"Beaver. What the fuck are you doing in here?"

"Gimme that," I say. "You're not doing that."

"Man who the fuck are you anyway?"

"Gimme that can."

"You fuck off," he says, "and nobody will even have to know you were here."

Think . . .

He says, "My uncle will appreciate it."

. . . Burn the house, convince her to sell?

"You got five seconds to get."

. . . Who even blew the hose?

With the flashlight in my eyes and Jarrod stepping close it occurs to me how this could all work out, how I could have a secret, like currency, how I could exchange it, turn it in to some supervisor job, the way Ernesto used to run a processor back in the old days, and how this type of shady shit is what it takes to get ahead, and I got what it takes, right? I'm an industrious motherfucker. I proved it with that nail in Jarrod's boot and I say, "Look, Jarrod. Just chill. We're cool."

He's in my face now.

"We're cool, man."

His posture softens. He says good, his lighter's dead anyway. I reach in my pocket for mine and you can call it a conscience, or you can call it impulsive behavior, or you can call it just being a real fucking chaos monster, but instead of forking it over, I tell him how one night on my break I faked having the shits and I snuck over to his shack and I took a nail from the skirting of the shower house and pushed it into his boot.

"The whole time I was doing it, I could hear you snoring," I tell him.

The beam in my eyes and this whizzing sound, a bomb in my ear, and I don't know, the floor, my spinning head, grunting, the sharp toes in my ribs and I'm curling up, curled up, too much body to protect at one time, cover the head, get it in the stomach, cover the stomach, and there's another in the neck, oh fuck he's got more hands and feet than me, like an ant, like a Hindu God or something, and I see my bones scorched in the rubble, and I'm screaming fuck you, because fuck him, and now I'm screaming STOP, and now someone is screaming PLEASE, and I swear it's not me, it's someone else, I swear it.

"What the fuck?"

A tiny red light, a fucking pixie, dancing around Jarrod's head and he's swatting at it, noise and feet shuffling, smacking fists, and the red light hits the floor, and the cherry breaks apart across the floorboards and now I've got the flashlight and see Bayram getting beat by Jarrod and that coffee cup finds my hand, and it only takes one swing, one that counts, not at his face, but through it. Then one more, two maybe, three at most, before Bayram's pulling me off.

Out cold, Jarrod's nose is broken so bad it looks like somebody's tried to erase it from a sketch of his face. There's blood bubbling from the flap where the yellow bone protrudes.

"Is he dead?"

"That was excessive!" Bayram says. "We could have just tackled him or something."

Jarrod gasps, starts to groan.

"Thank God," Bayram says.

Behind him, the cushions are on fire.

Thirty-Eight

"We need to get him back to the processor," Bayram says.

I think, do we? But I say okay.

We help him up, steady him on the way out. By the time we get him through the window, the back wall of the house is crackling and orange. Outside it's sprinkling but not hard enough.

"Where'd he go?" Jarrod mumbles. "It wasn't a fair fight."

I say, "I think some fisherman did it."

"Yeah," Bayram says. "Some unknown fisherman."

At the office, I tell Heather that some fishermen attacked him and we found him in the woods. We sit him down on an office chair, where I can see that one eye's swollen shut.

Outside, Bayram says, "We are so fucked."

I say, "It was dark. We couldn't see what happened."

He just stares at me.

"Say that for me, Bay."

"It was dark and we could not see."

"Some fisherman attacked him."

"Some fisherman attacked him."

"It was really dark."

"This is stupid, Beaver. We are fucked."

"He was over there trying to burn the house," I say. "If he says what happened, he'll be admitting to it."

Thirty-Nine

I pass out and follow maps upstream. Maps somebody left me a
long time ago. Watch me wiggle and grind against the current.
There's a net. There's a talon. A bone, a skull. It doesn't hurt to
dissolve. Not like you'd think. I can smell my own meat going
sour. Genetic rot. At least my body feeds the watershed: Lion
King shit, concentric circles. The freezers, the glaciers. The processor, the riverbank. The fish are the river and now I'm swimming against them. My face to the jaws, their pinprick teeth,
their bright eyes. What if I just swam until I came apart? Is it
raining? I can hear it whipping across the bunkhouse windows.
Falling like a carwash over the aluminum roof.

"Wake up."

Bayram's lying on Smitty's cot, a cigarette between his lips,
his hands crossed on his chest, corpselike, XTRATUFs hanging
off the bed, clods of last night's mud on the floor. He's soaking
wet. The morning puts last night back together. The nose, the
fire. Toward the other side of the room a few guys are sleeping
with T-shirts laid over their eyes. This isn't even Bayram's bunkhouse. It's already after noon. I sit up.

"Did they come for you too?"

There's sand in my hair. I say, "Who?"

"The authorities. It figures they would find me first."

"What'd they say? We didn't do anything wrong."

Bayram drops his cigarette in a sawed-off pop can on the floor. "It does not matter. It was the same officer from before, on the slime line."

"Bayram this isn't our fault."

"It's not *my* fault," he says.

Somebody yells at us to shut up.

He says, "They already had a whole narrative made. Jarrod was assaulted by some fisherman. But you and I, we were in the bear house. People saw us walking over there. They said I must have been careless with a cigarette."

"That's fucking stupid," I say. "Nobody will believe that."

"Everybody believes it. We walked right past everyone."

Somebody yells shut up again. Bayram stands.

I say I'm sorry. I say I'll get it sorted out.

I say wait but he doesn't. He doesn't say anything. He just slouches away.

Forty

No cops came looking for me before my shift and now I'm in the processor, standing at the bottom of the catwalk steps, gnawing at my brain for solutions. What to do, now, with Kevin? I know what I saw in the bear house. I know what we did. But what does Kevin know? Maybe I knocked the whole night out of Jarrod's brain and now he thinks he lit the fire and then fought some fisherman. Either way, Kevin knows it wasn't us who lit the house. He wanted the house burned, no shit, but the burst hose? I keep flipping the questions, holding them up to the fluorescent lights above me, trying to see new angles. Sometimes dumb is the best way to play it. It's what people expect from me.

It's like the time I got sent to Mr. Pritchard after I defiled a computer mouse belonging to a sworn enemy of Nick Destin. But when I got caught in the act, with jeans around my ankles and my book bag still high on my back, Nick shared none of the blame. It was practically his idea. He practically made me! My punishment was in-school suspension, a handwritten apology, mandatory counseling. After the word got around, everyone would whisper and laugh when I zipped up my trapper keeper to leave math for our meetings.

On our first meeting, I tried some of my usual tricks. The problem people have with skirting consequence is that they settle on one approach—very sorry or very stupid. It's better to spread yourself thin. Become very sorry *and* very stupid, which makes you sorry for being stupid. And people pity the dumb. Back before we knew I was just misaligned, my teachers loved me. You poor little dipshit. Have they tested the water over in Laurel Lane? Have you been snacking on paint chips?

Pritchard checked my bullshit. "Well, which is it?" he said. "Did your judgment lapse or don't you know any better? It can't be both."

No one else has ever asked me that. The truth is I'm still not sure.

From the catwalk, I can see the processor limping along. The first tender of the day was half empty and now, low on fish, running a skeleton crew, even the machines look sad. The header and gutter chasing its own tail. The try-hard slime line doing nothing. I notice for the first time that the tin walls are sky blue. The lights that hang from the rafters look like trashcans. There are two huge Alaskan flags hanging from the wall in packing, next to a stack of empty fish totes that go clear to the ceiling. The strip curtains are still. The forklifts are quiet. Helen's pulling racks for the only packing line working. I watch her work, try to think instead of feel, but fail.

Earlier, I thought about splitting. Hitch to Paulson, take the first flight out of here. But how would I even get my paycheck? They're holding all my money, everything since herring season. I couldn't even afford a ticket and stuck is stuck is stuck, and I knock on the cheap plywood door, and stuck is stuck, and my room and board, and Kevin grunts. He's sitting at his metal desk wearing a Klak Fancy hat and a Klak Fancy fleece. There's literally nothing on the desk but his hands, like big pink grapefruits, and a copy of the *Anchorage Daily News*. I'd imagined a computer, a stack of clipboards, shipping charts, rolodexes. I'd imagined old photos of the plant, Ernesto building bunkhouses. The emptiness terrifies me. It feels like an interrogation booth.

"I'm Garrett," I say. "I helped get Jarrod back to the cannery after his assault."

He snorts just like some kind of animal, and it's obvious he knows everything.

He says, "That's right. The Beaver. I need coffee. Would you like any?"

"If you're having some."

"I just fucking said I was having some."

He stands and leaves and this feels like those first few meetings with Mr. Pritchard, the way he'd pull the same trick, leaving me alone in the office like this. But now Kevin's across from me again, and the cup is in my hand. The Styrofoam squeaks. I can hear it in my nerves. It feels like I'm at the edge of a very high place.

"What's so funny?"

I say nothing, level my face. He points like I was reading his
newspaper, the president on the front page.

"What do you think?" he says. "W?"

It takes me a minute to get it. "Oh," I say. "I'm not very
political."

"I don't care for silver-spoon types," he says. "It breaks my
heart that the Democrats are such pussies. But the Republicans
want to turn Alaska into Swiss cheese. Drill this, mine that.
They want to put a copper mine at the headwaters of the fishery.
Can you believe that?"

"Unbelievable," I say.

"Funny thing now, holding hands with the hippies and the
Natives. We got mines pushing in on us, goddamn dyed-fake-red
fucking farmed salmon cutting in on our market, destroying our
fisheries. Then there's OSHA, and fucking quality control. And
I can't even get foreign labor with all the new terrorism security
stuff. Every three years we got to look to some new shitty part of
the Earth to find people willing to work."

I sip, burn my tongue, try not to pant. There's a fancy ulu in
a marble rack on the shelf behind Kevin and it's obvious it's never
touched a fish. But a throat? Because that's what we're doing
here, right? So obvious when I just think, when I take the time
to think, and he says—

"Then this business with my nephew." He's leaning on his
hands, talking through his fingers. "Kid's always starting fights.
He just doesn't usually lose them. We couldn't find anything
about the fisherman who beat him." He looks me up and down,
nods at my shirtsleeve pulled over my bruised hand.

He says, "He must've been a huge guy, that fisherman. Jarrod doesn't remember a thing. Just a bad concussion, broken nose. He's already back in Anchorage getting his nose fixed. I guess that'll be my fucking bill to pay, too."

He pulls his hands down from his face. His rings scrape on the desk. Chalkboard-like, setting my teeth on edge.

"His dad sent him up here, thinking it'll build him character."

"I think working here does build character," I say. "Or it can."

"You can't build something without materials though, can you? And that kid's got no lumber or concrete or nothing. He's already practically ruined with entitlement."

"That's terrible."

"It's lucky you found him."

I nod, wait him out.

He says, "No matter what I do, I can't stop kids from trespassing over there at Otis's place. I've tried everything. Even before this, that place needed condemned. It's a safety risk. If it'd been dry out, that fire could've spread to the processor. Burned up the whole boatyard, everything. We're damn lucky it happened to be a wet night."

"Damn lucky," I say. "But Bayram and I didn't burn it. You know that."

"I doubt you did it on purpose. Just two drunk kids, careless with their cigarettes."

"I don't even smoke," I tell him. "Maybe it was Jarrod."

"Now, think," he says. "How could it have been Jarrod if you found him in the woods all beaten up?"

He's right.

I say, "I'll tell you I did it if that's what you want. But Bayram didn't do shit."

He sighs, says, "Is that what you think this is? There's no jury here. Here I thought you were gung-ho on becoming a foreman."

"I am."

But oh shit, the churning parts of me are saying I'm not.

"You gonna be sick?"

There's a compass in my stomach and it's starting to spin.

I say I'm fine and he takes off his hat. He's bald on the top with a horseshoe of thick, black hair. His face is stubbly and sallow. He looks at the paper and says, "I heard about some issue at the Black Dog before the fish started running."

Gulp.

"And despite that," he says. "Despite all of that, I had you penciled in to take Helen's job. Fuck, maybe even Ernesto's job, once we start shuffling everybody to expand. I was even hoping you could get Bonnie to sit down and talk. That bitch won't even look at me. But all that's over."

He stands up and now he's sitting on the edge of his desk, looking down at me. You can tell he does this all the time. He never raises his voice. That's the worst part. He doesn't have to. He says, "We're expanding. We *need* to expand. If you're not growing, you're shrinking."

I tell him I'm not certain what he's asking me to do.

"I'm not asking you to do anything," he says. "There's nothing you can do. What, you're gonna go say that my nephew burned down the house, it was all one big set-up, and you and your buddy just happened to get in the way? You're gonna say the two of you broke his nose, busted up his head, and that's self-defense? You, the guy who works for the woman whose house was burned, alongside one of the guys starting trouble at my processor all summer? Both of you already on the local cops' shit list? You, some fucking weirdo all strung out on who-knows-what?"

He says, "We're not negotiating. Either you fuck off, or you go back to work until we're done for the season, and then you get paid and fuck off. That's it. That's the best outcome. You're getting a pretty square deal."

I tell him I could call the department of labor on him and he slaps the desk with both hands so hard that the fat on his face ripples and slowly settles again.

He says, "I refuse to be the bad guy here. I just won't accept it. I'm just a little fish and the sea's full of them. Do you hear me?"

He looks at his big watch. "I got another meeting. It's hell, running a business."

Forty-One

I jump the three steps to Bayram's trailer and swing open the door and see nothing. The cots are stripped, blankets folded and stacked, ashtrays emptied, windows propped open. It reeks of cigarettes and cologne and mildew. They can keep the windows open all winter if they want. That smell's never coming out.

Bayram's gone. What else is there left to do,

But, work?

Stuck is the yaba in my nose and stuck is the heat in my head and stuck is the feeling that the more I want to do right by people the more I think it's impossible, and stuck's the twelver I volunteer for—racks, racks, racks, stuck in the ice, then unstuck—because what else is there to do? It's so much easier to live when you're empty and stupid and safe in the cold cocoon of the freezer, and when Helen finally pushes me out the door, I learn that Bayram got spooked and told the cops that he'd been smoking in the bear house, and they drove him straight to the airport.

It could be worse, Sven said.

And now I'm wandering around looking for Bonnie thinking about why people always say that *it could be worse*, instead of saying it could be better.

It could be worse—Bayram could have gotten into legal trouble.

It could be worse—this could be a copper mine.

It could be worse—this is the most sustainable fishery on Earth.

It could be worse—salmon everywhere else are dying.

It could be worse—I could be snorting meth or something sketchy, something dangerous, I could have cancer or a real addiction, a real illness, not this made-up mental shit! Eat up, Garrett, there's starving kids somewhere! I remember the smell of my mom's menthols, two packs a day, and I saw the fuel slick on the water in that picture of my dad, and last night in the bar all the fishermen were just focused on getting back to work, focused on their bills, and who can blame them, but it all feels related and it's hard to say how. Look. I know I'm supposed to compare my problems to the grand scheme of things, but what does that do other than separate your pain from my pain? Just shame, pushing pain down deeper, down where it rots—

What I mean is that what people call the grand scheme of things is just the sum of all our tiny schemes, right? What I mean is that there are lots of other actions we ought to be defining as suicidal, and I think Bonnie will get it, she has to, and I run down to her shack and see her locking the door on her way out. Her hands are stained gray, and her boots are ashy, and she smells like mildew and smoke. There's a look on her face I've never seen on a person before, like her face is in a denser gravity. Sag and defeat, and underneath it, the relief that defeat brings.

"You broke into the house?" she says, like she's trying to scream but can't. "After everything I told you, you and your fucking friends go in there and burn it all down?"

I say let me explain, let me explain, let me explain.

Even after she's gone, I stand there repeating it.

The Klak Fancy Letter
Friday, July 21st

Hello Folks,

Due to economic forces outside of our control, we've made the decision to reduce our workforce a little earlier than usual. Accordingly, we'll be moving all workers into Bunkhouses A and B. Just find an empty bunk and make it your own.

I also want to say that I am mad as hell about the behavior of some of our workers during the recent closure. Each and every one of you represents Klak Fancy—and, by extension, me!—and I don't like my name sullied because my workers cannot hold their liquor. Rest assured that the workers responsible for the recent acts of vandalism have been sent packing!

Important Updates:

*Laundry Service is suspended for the rest of the season.

Fish Count: 232,290

Weather: High of 66, sun. Sunrise—5:53 a.m. Sunset—11:12 p.m.

Alaska Word of the Day: Adventure—An unusual, exciting, and **risky** journey or event. I like to say that the A in Alaska is for Adventure. **Even if you come here looking to make a quick buck, the experience is worth more than gold.**

Forty-Two

I wait for her at her shack but she doesn't come. Before my shifts, after, I just sit there under the eave, watching the workers leave. HARD WORKER and girlfriend and a few dozen others are let go, and two days after the fire, we're down to just Americans and Ernesto's crew. A good late run of fish comes, then. A week of solid hours. The kind of money that could have put Bayram in the black. The biologists say it has something to do with quickly changing water temperatures. The salmon wait for cool weather and rain to run, and this year they had to wait a little longer. It's possible that the warmer lakes are even making things better for the smolts. But the Yukon runs are so bad they've suspended all commercial fishing. Copper River Kings aren't much better. With the Turks gone, and the Moldovans gone, and the Colombians gone, it's hard to keep up. But I do. I pull racks so fast that I get told to slow down. I skip my breaks, what use are breaks, fuck breaks. Helen asks if I am acting weird because of what happened between us.

"What are you talking about?"

"Garrett, your nose is bleeding."

"Freezer's cold," I tell her and later that shift I remember this one time when Bonnie took me to the boat shop in Klak to get line. At the checkout, she told me to go to the little café behind the shop and get her a peanut butter milkshake. It wasn't much more than a coffee stand with a hot plate and the woman at the window was sad looking with a shark's tooth necklace overtop her black T-shirt. She said, "A peanut butter milkshake. This isn't for Bonnie Kohle, is it?"

I paused. Something in her tone. I said no and the milkshake followed. I took a long pull from the straw to really sell it. Brain freeze. Bonnie'd told me a few days before that brain freeze is what it feels like to drown, but in your whole body at once.

Things could be worse—

. . . His ass

. . . His ass

. . . His ass.

In the parking lot, I told Bonnie what happened and she laughed. She said, "That's Kate. She hates me because she thinks I was fucking her husband."

"Why's she think that?"

"Because she caught me fucking her husband." She took three long drinks from the milkshake and asked if I wanted any. I didn't. On the way out of the lot, she rolled down the window and lobbed the shake and it exploded on the windshield of a purple minivan.

"Bullseye," she said. We launched a rainbow of gravel peeling out onto the road. "The nerve of some people. Why does she think she gets to grudge me like that? I never agreed to be responsible for her feelings."

It's hard to know who you owe, and how much. But I want to know. I want to pay it back. In the meantime, I just pull racks. At the end of my shift, I smash my middle finger in a rack so hard my fingernail falls off. I find it in my glove and hold it for a long time, like there's a way to put it back together. In the end, I just stick it in the pocket of my freezer suit to leave a piece of myself behind for some kid next year to find and worry about.

Forty-Three

The fish stop, cleanup starts.

The final *Klak Fancy Letter* says to go to the chow house at 8 p.m., where, I'm sure, Kevin and the Klak cop will be waiting to haul me away. No one will testify to my character. Facebook reveals my criminal poop. My mom wears white to the courthouse. She's standing there next to Bonnie and they look a lot alike. The same knowing faces. Smug in the lips, disappointment on the brow. Bayram behind the pulpit in a powdered wig, red fox on his shoulder. The perp walk through the sand and I swing open the final doors and see the hall full of foremen and the last of the processor crew. The heavy smell of pizza. There's an enormous stack of them and coolers of pop and a tray of cookies the size of a toddler. Kevin herds us all into a line and we load up paper plates. While we eat, he stands in the front of the room and thanks us all for our hard work and for our loyalty, our loyalty, our loyalty, our loyalty, our loyalty, and he adds that the processor can't function without people like us. We are the lifeblood of the fishing industry. The fishermen get all the credit, all the newspaper stories and reality TV shows, but it's us who turn fish into food. He tells us to look out in the winter. Some of us will be invited back to salaried positions.

I distend myself with three Cokes, three cookies, and three slices of pizza. On the fourth, I start to feel sick so I return it to the box with a bite taken out. I suck the sauce from my fingers but it won't come clean. I lick again, remember my missing fingernail.

Fooled, again!

The chow house empties. On the way out, Helen hands me two brown envelopes and keeps walking. There's a Post-it on one that says, *Bayram's mail. Got no way to get it to him.*

The iPods. He had them shipped here.

I sit and wait and watch some workers kiss Kevin's taint. By the time he's free, everyone else has left. Why the pageantry? Just drop the curtain, reveal the ruse. Haul me away. I'm helping clean up pizza boxes. I tie off a trash bag, slap open another. He turns and sees me.

"What?"

"I didn't say shit," I say. "In case you're wondering. Just wanted to tell you."

"I know," he says, tapping his temple to say he hasn't forgotten. "It wouldn't matter anyway. Your buddy leaned in *real* hard. Saved his friends their room and board in the process."

And I know that should make me feel better, but it doesn't. He's walking around looking for the light switches and with every step he takes, he shrinks a little more. He used to be strong, you can see it in his frame, but now he's all slack and flub. The creases of his neck like folded lunchmeat. A sad sack of cells, a polo shirt turned flesh and blood. It'd be so easy to rush him and hit him and hit him and hit him until I could peel back his mask. I feel my blood clobbering my eardrums.

It'd be so easy.

Sand—

The time comes.

The time goes.

He takes the door to the plant, his plant, and is gone. I'm all alone in the chow house with one dying fluorescent bulb buzzing above me, and it occurs to me that this is the part when I'm supposed to do something. Rage, or cry, or change, or something. But for a minute I'm just stuck, physically this time, glued to the floor with the weight of everything that could happen next.

A pair of mice run across the floor and a feeling comes, something heavy and calm, the look on Bonnie's face—I could walk into the sea and maybe only three or four people on the planet would even know the difference. There's a freedom in that, a sort of untouchability, and I take the packages and go to leave, but those mice are chattering at one corner of the room, by a pile of crumbs, and when I bend down to see them, there's something black by Kevin's chair where his jacket had been. A worn leather trifold wallet, still damp from his fat ass.

So here I am, at the season's end, alone in the rain under a moon-colored motion light, leaning against the chain-link fence surrounding the holding tank full of blood and milt and sea water. Kevin's official address is 440 Holyoke Ave, Seattle, Washington. His age is sixty-four. He is five-foot-eleven, two hundred and ten pounds. Brown eyes. He plans to donate his organs. Here are his bank cards, he uses Wells Fargo. His business cards, other people's business cards, phone numbers, passwords, a single grainy photo of who I assume are his parents, a blank piece of cardstock that reads, in thick pen—

Fisherman's Prayer

God grant that I may live to fish for another
  shining day.
But when my final cast is made I then most
  humbly pray,
When nestled in your landing net, As I lay
  peacefully asleep,
You'll smile and judge that I'm good enough to
  keep.

Here is eight hundred and twenty-four dollars. There it goes into my pocket.

And there go the basic facts of one man's life, sinking into the chum.

The Second Part

So there's this baby fur seal, and he walks into this bar
and grabs a seat.

And the bartender says, "What'll you have?"

And the seal says, "I like whisky. What you got?"

And the bartender, he says, "We got Jack Daniels and we got Jim
Beam and we got Northern Lights and we got Canadian Club."

The seal jumps up from his seat. "Canadian Club?" he cries.
"That's the drink that killed my brother."

One

The first thing worth noticing is the stuffed and mounted bear at the airport. It's a polar bear, sleek and white and nautical, like a seal from a nightmare, like a murder-seal, nine feet tall on its back legs in a glass case outside of the terminal. Catcher's mitt–sized paws, claws the length of fingers. The plaque says it was shot to death in downtown Nome in 1986 after killing seven sled dogs. I don't think a dog's life is as valuable as a human life, but hypothetically, how many? I'm wondering because of the family posing for photos. This soccer mom is at the camera and finance dad is holding a little boy wearing a polar bear shirt by the waist to get the boy's head closer to the bear's. Dad's arms are shaking. He lifts the boy higher, tilts him at his mother's instruction so that it looks like the bear is poised to crush the kid inside its black mouth.

Welcome to Anchorage.

Sven and Smitty took the same plane as me out of Klak but now I've lost them. It's all tourists and fishermen, people in a hurry, loud in a way I didn't even realize I'd forgotten. I wander around looking for them, then I'm outside. It's warmer than

Klak and it smells like exhaust. It's a different kind of dirty. The dirt of thousands of people living. I see all the pavement, and all the cars, and it hits me that Klak Fancy really is over for me. I find the taxiway and see Sven slipping into a yellow cab. I call him, no answer, and a few minutes later he texts: *My bad man. I'm crashing at a friend's pad no room for three.* In a few days, he's going to a music festival up North. That's all I know about anyone from the plant. Everyone else just peace'd. It's not like there were yearbooks to sign.

I take a cab down Northern Lights, past the Taco Bells and the auto garages and the fur wholesalers and the Fred Meyer with a half dozen eagles shitting intermittently on the sign. Things I'd forgotten about are starting to come back to me, like the crosswalk buttons at G State. I'd never even seen one before, and my first week of college I stood at a crosswalk for ten minutes, waiting. Nobody believes me when I tell them that story. I told it at a party once and somebody said it was rude to make fun of rural people like that.

Things I like are coming back, too. Taco Bell. The smell of the bread outside of Subway. The rainbow streaked on a car windshield from a gas station squeegee. This is my first time in a taxi and it'd be alright to stay in one forever, away from the feeling of being out in the world with all the people moving in different directions, and all at once someone looks at you and the rest of your day is a question mark about what stupid thing you were doing to cause that look. What can they see that I can't? I was at the edge of foresight there for a minute, for a month. It was like the future was unfurled for me. But here, the sidewalk's still bloody. My sores are breaking open again.

I get taken to midtown, where they keep the payday lenders and the hostels and the hardware supply stores. In the cab my phone rings and I let it ring. There's a voicemail from the Klak police department, asking me to return their call Re: information regarding theft and criminal vandalism at Klak Fancy Salmon, LLC.

Delete.

I book two nights at the Arctic Adventure Hostel and the place is swimming with drunk fishermen and drunk foreign processor workers and one blond mountaineer with a bruise on his cheek, swollen and split like an overripe tomato. He's sitting at a picnic table on the hostel's patio, working on his tattered feet with medical tape. They're beyond fucked. Foot is hardly even the right word anymore. The pinky toe is curved so hard it's practically a rotini. The toenail faces downward. The space in between is the color of sauce. He clips off dead skin with small scissors and tosses it into the wind.

"Why mountains?" I ask him.

He looks up. "As opposed to what?" He has a British accent.

"I don't know. As opposed to oceans."

"You can't climb a fucking ocean, mate."

Thinking maybe it's about time to try.

Just swim.

Two

Yaba and a forty. Anchorage is big but the internet is bigger. How does something so big move so fucking fast? It just keeps coming at me from my seat at a grimy desktop in the public library, a brutal concrete building with about fifty homeless people moving around. I'm waiting around for messages because I spent the morning sleuthing online. Bayram, turns out, is a common name. But I found a Facebook group called KLAK IS WHACK 2006. I swore never again with Facebook, but I did it. There was no choice. I logged in and was slapped with hundreds of notifications from March. There were entire G State groups devoted to the mystery upper decker. Someone kept tagging me in pictures of dogshit they took across campus. Dozens of people had posted on my wall asking if it was me, sending praises and threats. I thought about my mom. All our mutual connections online. She had to have seen the posts on my wall. She probably wasn't surprised. I can see the corners of her mouth tick up. The frown mistaken for a smile.

I left a comment on the Klak group saying I was looking for Bayram. There were a couple members with Turkish names. One, I knew, was a part of his crew.

Now there's a line forming behind me and I can feel their hot eyes on the back of my neck. "Wait," I say to the guy tapping on my shoulder, telling me my computer time's up. I hand him twenty bucks of Kevin's. I tell him just five minutes and that's when the idea comes. The dumbfuck's Gmail password was in his wallet: S0ckI-69. But now the people in line behind me want paid, too, and I'm handing out tens, and the librarian is scolding me, and she's not accepting my money, and why am I bleeding, Sir, stick a tissue in your nose at least, Sir. Sir, we're going to have to ask you to leave.

One minute.

Sir, I'm going to have to call security if you keep handing out money like this—

I knock out a few quick lines about processing bad fish on the beach and a few more about the bear house fire and one about eating raw salmon as a cure for ED and I grab about fifty contacts that look like buyers, and I hit send and jet before security comes.

Just ten minutes pass before I get a text from a number I don't know.

You stole my wallet didn't you???

I respond: *God grant that I may live to fish for another shining day. But when my final cast is made I then most humbly pray, When nestled in your landing net as I lay peacefully asleep, You'll smile and judge that I'm good enough to keep.*

*You little piss ant fuck you're never going to work in this
industry again I have nothing but free time to fuck you I've been
stomping on little toads like you my whole life.*

I send him the fisherman's prayer again and take a cab
downtown and I ask the driver what is and isn't my fault and
can't be sure if he hears me so I buy fifteen Big Macs with Kevin's money and walk around trying to give them to homeless
people. In Anchorage, I learn, the homeless stick to the tourist
spots downtown, the districts with the street carts selling rein-
deer sausage and the souvenir shops each with a stuffed bear
out front. I also learn that the people of Anchorage are incredu-
lous about free Big Macs. One young Native woman takes one
kindly and I watch her toss it into a trashcan. I eat two of them
and then try to hand the paper sacks to a very small old white
man wearing a winter coat that's as greasy as the bags. He
looks me dead in the eyes, and his skin is wrinkled, you can
practically palm-read his face, there are codes embedded there,
and his expression is so shameless, and he's saying words and
those words are, "Young man, who do you think you're helping
with this shit?"

I stuff the rest of Kevin's money into his coat and pretend
not to hear him shouting at me while I cross the busy street
and break into a sprint.

Blurred sidewalks and office parks and eventually I wash up
at some nightlife district along the waterfront. There's an upscale
wine bar with jazz leaking from the open door. I think about
Bonnie. Out front on a bench, near a belligerent magpie, a young
blonde woman in a gold dress is gently crying. She asks for a

lighter. Her purse looks very expensive, and her face looks a little like Helen's and the bird seems mystified by her dress. It bobs its head like a boxer, moving in toward her, then retreating.

She says, "What the fuck are you staring at?"

I say, "Are you crying because of your haircut?"

And now she is crying harder and throwing rocks at me and soon I'm riding back to the hostel in a taxi. We're stopped at a red light when I see Sven and Smitty walking out of some place called the Moose's Tooth with a box of pizza.

"Let me out here."

Three

They were surprised to see me. They asked if I was lost. They said what's up with the clothes. I was still in my work hoodie and boots. I said the same thing back. They brought extra clothes to Alaska?

They did!

They'd rented a car and were leaving for a road trip up North and didn't have a ton of room. I said I'd buy the booze and they said and maybe the gas? We picked up my shit and got a cheap tent and drove, past the part of the city where they keep the strip clubs and fireworks stands and the used car lots with those creepy inflatable men seizing in the wind. Then, the inlet to the left and mountains to the right. We were hardly out of the city when we crossed the biggest river I'd ever seen. Braids and braids of it. It was violent. The water was as thick as milk. It looked like stomach medicine. Sven said it was full of silt, rocks pulverized by glaciers. I didn't know Alaska at all.

And now, at the festival gate, another Alaska. Sven and Smitty and I are standing in line behind some hippies wearing tails. Fox tails, red and tipped black. Silvery wolf tails. Neon-blue tails, pink tails, one covered with jewels and another threaded with blinking Christmas lights, tied to their belts or pinned to their pants, and one that's sewn to the waistband of a tattered pink tutu worn by a big husky guy with mutton chops and a black leather jacket with one arm spray-painted gold. He's the man in charge of the gate, standing behind a foldout card table with a box of cash and a packet of wristbands.

He says, "You cops?"

"What?" Sven says. "We're not cops."

He laughs and his teeth are very green. "I ask everyone. If you're a cop, you legally have to tell me."

"Actually, I don't think that's true."

He says, "No guns, no glass, no fighting. Camp anywhere. Use the hot tubs. My name's Denim. You see anyone with a pink tutu, they're volunteers, they can help you out. Cops patrol the highway for miles, but this is private land. We keep it under four hundred people, and technically it's just a big party. Can't come in without a warrant."

Smitty says, "I love this state."

Sven says, "An enlightened people."

We follow the tails down the skinny dirt road to the festival with the black spruce leeching mosquitos around us. It's warm here, hot almost. Windless, dank, and buggy. I ask Sven what's up with the tails.

"It's just some festival thing. You got a girl back home in Ohio?"

"Pennsylvania."

"Whichever."

"Nope," I say. There was Kaleigh, sophomore year of high school, an evangelical who gave dry hand jobs. And Mel, freshman year of college. She liked to cut herself but only on her thighs. I felt the raised checkerboard above her knees in the dark and had no idea what to say. She texted me one time: *Just thought of ur cock and now I'm sitting in a puddle in the middle of calc.* After that, I couldn't see her again. It was just too embarrassing.

"I did hook up with Helen, though," I say.

"I know. She told me."

"What?"

Smitty goes, "Nice."

Sven says, "Helen and I are cool. We used to date. Well, date's not the term."

"What's the term?"

"Sexual congress."

And now I feel low.

Sven's big festival takes place in some clearing, a sandy pit lined with green Port-a-John's ripe with shit. A stage at one end, roofed with a flapping canvas tarp, and a couple trucks selling coffee, tie-dye, pipes, tacos, whatever. The hot tubs are actually just steel cattle troughs, stacks of wood next to them. We walk the narrow roads that circle the stage, past a few teepees made from spruce poles and blue tarps, past a man dressed as a wizard, another wearing foam horns on his head and a flute hanging on his hairy chest. Past bros slamming beers near their trucks, past RVs, past tents, past a spruce tree decorated with condoms in plastic bags and a sign that says FREE LOVE FREE ALASKA FREE FISH, past a woman with long brown braids, tits out, past kids with rainbows on their faces, past a row of worn-out XTRATUFs with flowers planted inside, past dogs, collarless dogs, unneutered, balls swinging.

We find a spot and set up camp.

Later, in my palm, the mushrooms Sven buys with my money don't look like much. Just brown hunks, rimmed in blue. They smell like dirt. I'm remembering the first time I got stoned, at my mom's family reunion. They were rednecks. They are, I mean—fireworks, guns, four-wheelers I was never taught how to ride. I walked down some train tracks with my older cousins. We punched holes in a pop can with a safety pin. "You don't get high the first time." A few minutes after, my voice circled my head and came back to my ears like it was carrying a fucking olive branch. I remember drawing in the hot railroad tar with my thumb. My mouth like I'd gargled wet bread. I tried telling my mom we'd been wrestling and I got dirt in my eyes. A couple weeks later, she introduced me to Officer Flex. He showed me a photo he took of four kids dead in a high-speed collision.

Maybe I should join the army.

I down them. Bitter.

We sit in the dirt and I tell Sven and Smitty about the iPods. Smitty says it's Bayram's own fault for being so naive, like the time he got mugged giving a guy a ride home.

"I get that," I say. "But that still doesn't make it right."

"But you just want to feel better," Sven says. "Everything we do is self-motivated."

"So if I feel better, and he gets his stuff back, that's wrong?'

He stands up. "I can't talk about this with somebody who hasn't taken any philosophy."

Apparently, we're all standing up now because the ground's further away.

"My guys," Smitty says. "Good vibes only."

At the pit some terrible band is playing. They have a banner that says FUCK WAR and for a second I can't remember which one. Sven puts his arm around me and he says, "You need to know the rules." *Rules.* Fear reaches up to grab me, pinching at my ankles. "Listen," he says. His face is taking up my whole screen. "Don't look in any mirrors. Also, don't look at your dick. If anything upsets you, just walk away."

"And don't eat any spaghetti," Smitty adds.

"Where would he find spaghetti?" Sven says.

But what if I already ate some spaghetti and forgot? What if I need to look at my dick?

Uh, oh—

The singer's wearing a costume like a zebra. The one with the banjo has an American flag for a cape. They play a song, then another, which means that around us time is happening. Next to Sven, Smitty's making mush with his lips, barely language. I don't see anything worth saying. The song is ending. The song has ended. People cheer. They should know better. What now? In the lull, dark forces move through my fingers, my penis. Piss. I keep checking but always come up dry. My heart knocks on the door to itself but the knocking is muffled by piss. Someone is next to me. Sven is next to me, Smitty is next to Sven. These are people I know. Say it like an incantation. Friends, drums. With these two friends, the new song feels nice in my body. The drums drum in my teeth. It turns out I can breathe and I do it very well.

"Beaver," Sven says. That is my name!

"A tail," I say. "A flat tail I can smack against the water to alert us of danger."

"You're just so stupid!"

Four

The three of us in the tent and I'm trying to eat a potato chip. The sandpaper edges, the pill-sized salt. I've never tasted something so bad. I say so and Smitty gives me a little pill. Then, another. Sven tells us we ought to chill with those.

"Really," Sven says. "That's a combo I do not . . ."

"Shh," I tell him. "How stupid do you think I am?"

"You thought you found a leg," he says, giggling. "That's how fucking stupid you are." He adjusts a Maglite against the walls of the tent, brighter and dimmer. When the aperture opens, I see my smallness at the edge of the void. Music in the distance, dogs barking, and shadows on the tent walls possibly maybe probably something with teeth, skulking. The feeling of something with very large teeth. Who is panting?

"You thought you were going to run the processor," Smitty says.

"Yeah, you and Helen!"

"Maybe we should get out of here," I say.

"You can't," Sven says. "You know?"

"Not forever. Just for now."

The light keeps swelling and receding. Like an asshole or an eye. Helen's pine knots, watching. What did she tell him? What could he know? I don't feel so good.

"Please stop."

He does not.

I try to take the flashlight and he bops me on the head with it.

"Relax."

"The tent's melting."

This kid from the trailer park got burnt by a plastic sled we tossed on a bonfire. They had to peel the plastic off his face! The plastic will outlive him. My mom will outlive me. "It's too fucking, fucking, fucking, fucking plastic in here," and now I'm on the road. The flowering boots, what happened to the owners? Something rotten inside of me, everything unbelonging, and I stop at a burning barrel circled by guys standing around. Their eyes are glowing, their cheeks are red. They're rotten, roasting, evil.

"Here man." There's something in my mouth. I watch the fire. Chew. Dry, bitter.

"Dude, no." He's pulling at my face. Dirty hands in my mouth. "You light it, dumbass." Everyone is laughing. They know about my dad. They know where I've shit. They know my many failures and I walk away.

Remembering what Sven said, I walk away from the next fire.

Remembering what Sven said, I walk away from the next fire.

Remembering what Sven said, I reach down to pet a dog, and it bites me in the hand.

The weather's really cold but my hand feels really warm. No one will take off their masks when I beg them. I flip open my phone, call my mom, tell her I'm at Nick Destin's house with a stomachache again and can she pick me up? I swear I'm not faking this time. I swear it really hurts. It hurts too bad to walk home and my phone is dead, and in the pit, a train whistles. The train plays the kind of songs that belong in graveyards. A man juggles torches in front of the stage. People clap, their breath in the air. My hand is sticky. He grabs me by my ankles and flips me from the balcony and now I'm falling through the trees, falling until the branches close in around me and the firelights are the size of stars.

Five

By the time I leave the woods my hand's throbbing like a motherfucker. Most of the barrel fires have gone out. The music's over and everything's staticky gray. I walk through a quiet camp, stumbling over tent lines, and at the road I see a threesome fucking in a hot tub, water roiling over the edges and sizzling on the red-eyed coals. A tangle of bodies, black hair fanned out in the water. A woman's head hangs over the edge of the tub, and she stares straight at me when she moans.

I find my tent, my flashlight. Two puncture wounds in my palm, another between my knuckles, and my thumbnail is black with blood. I douse it in water from a bottle, wrap it in a clean sock. It's all I can do. My tent flap is still open, my stuff spread out in the mud. I rake everything inside, zip the tent closed, accomplish something like sleep.

Then the tent's bright with light between the shadows of people walking by and I can hear kids laughing. A dog stops and pisses on my tent and when I slap the side, he jumps and runs away. Klak. My hand's been in an iron maiden. That's how it looks. Somehow nothing hurts but I can feel mosquito bites like pimples across my face. There's this image from last night that keeps coming back to me. In the woods, when the branches shook, I was on my back in the ocean at night. The ocean was electric. It was sending me emails. Little fish kept coming up to tug at me and my veins were outside of me and no one would look when I showed them. I just kept trying to show people. Why didn't they come and look for me?

"Yo," I say. "Sven."

Nothing.

"Hey Fuckers."

It takes a moment to process. I just keep looking to the dry patch of dirt where their tent sat and then back at mine. Everything I own is muddy, scattered in the tent. I throw my sleeping bag outside on a stump. I shake the pine needles from my hoodie. A knife, a toothbrush with no paste, dirty boxers. I close my eyes, demand myself to think. The pain comes howling in my hand.

Sven and Smitty. Those motherfuckers—

I'm running now, past the same flowering boots and tents and past all the dogs that could've bit me. The sock on my hand's turning pink and by the time I make it around the dirt road and back to the tent I've ditched it altogether. I start again. Even the weirdos are gawking. A little girl with clouds painted on her cheeks cuts in front of me and when we bump into each other I leave a little blood on the top of her head. I check the pit, the stage, the outhouses. I check the gate and find Denim.

"I've been robbed," I tell him. "Some fucking assholes stole my iPods."

He's got his big hands on my shoulders and his cowboy hat's shading both of us. "Shh, buddy," he says. "What happened to your hand?"

"Those two guys I came in with. They stole my fucking shit. Call the cops."

"Breathe, man. Just breathe."

Other volunteers around us now, a whole circle of tutus.

"Call the fucking cops."

"That's not an option."

Why are all these hands on me? Whose hands are these even? A flash of last night, hands in my mouth. Did I eat a cigarette? They're pushing me now, these guys in tutus, these girls with tails, and the harder I pull away, the more of them arrive, and they're pushing me back behind the stage and I'm sitting on a set of steps that leads to the stage and nobody's responding to anything I'm trying to tell them.

"I saw your friends driving out," Denim says. "Had to be three hours ago."

He's wearing a fur cape, and he pulls it off and puts it over my shoulders.

"You're shivering."

Denim's holding my hand, slowly turning it over in the light. I think of Helen. I can hear her moaning underneath Sven. I remember this looooong email I sent her in Anchorage and I want to throw up. I feel like dying. Denim's got an older face up close. I can see the black sprouts of hair on the end of his nose. I say I think I'm gonna be sick, and he points to the ground.

"Let her rip."

While I'm puking, he leaves and comes right back with some really jacked guy with a big camouflage bag slung over his shoulder. He's buzz-cut and sleeved in tattoos. Everyone keeps looking at me like I'm the weird one. "Yep," he says. "Canine." He turns my hand over, inspecting. "They don't have to be big to fuck you up."

He douses a clean towel with bottled water. "I'm Doug," he says.

Denim says Doug was a medic in Afghanistan.

A dirty woman in a tutu hands me a coffee and I thank her. Then, very gently, like I'm a little bird he's taken from the housecat, Doug cleans the dried blood from my hand while I swallow the urge to fall apart. He doesn't scrub, he dabs. He doesn't wipe, he pats.

"Well," Denim says. "Should we amputate?" He laughs.

"You'd be surprised how many dog bites I've treated," he says to me. "It was hardly ever strays, either. It was the pets that would freak when shelling got nuts."

"Don't get me wrong," Denim says. "I love dogs. But they know when you're high. Which dog was it?"

"He didn't say his name."

Peroxide, and gasping, and fresh white bandages.

"Puncture wounds are a real bitch to get clean. I'd recommend going to the doctor."

"Right."

He pulls a bottle of pills from the bag. "If I happened to drop like ten of these painkillers onto this step and you found them, you'd take them responsibly, right?"

Right.

He shakes a palmful from the bottle and slaps them onto the step. "Whoops."

I reach down to pick them up and things flip. My head in this soldier's lap. It's hardly even crying, just tears falling out of me. Just gravity. If I don't open my eyes I can't see the people looking at me. First, a small hand, not Doug's, light and soft. Then another's rubbing my back. There, there, buddy—all sorts of hushed voices. So many gentle hands. Every time a new one touches me, it gets worse. The weeping. I'm all curled up on the step, draped in a fur, wailing, and wailing, and wailing, and wailing, and when I wail, more people touch me, and the more that people touch me the louder I wail. I never knew there were so many hands. It's never felt this good to be so small. I can't remember the feeling of waking to my dad passed out in my bed holding me, but this I'll never forget. Please don't let me.

"Please," I say. Just so much snot. Snot and salt and the dirty step under my cheek, pebble dents on the side of my face.

"You just took too much."

"It happens to everybody."

"It happens to the best of us."

Beaver—

It is so good to hear that you have my iPods. All the phone calls I placed to try to find them led me nowhere. These last two weeks since my return have not been the best of my life. My sister told my mother that I lost her money in the United States and now the whole family is upset with me. My friends told everyone I misled them about Klak, hiding the referral money I received. That was my mistake, one I'm sure you understand considering the many you made this summer. I feel like my father now, the subject of so much gossip. Sometimes I wish I never came back. It makes me think of the time you told me you refused to go limping back to your home without any success.

But at least I was able to leave Klak without any criminal issues. You know how much I hate to lie but I had no choice. The stories I have told! But I think getting the iPods back will help in this regard. I can pay my sister back and at least we will be even. I may have to pause my schooling to get my finances in order. Go big or go home! America!

I looked into it and I think there will be no problem with you mailing them to me. Of course I cannot see myself returning to Alaska for work. It's great that it has worked out so well for you but there are many of us who saw nothing for our work.

Regards.

The Last Part

What's the difference between jam and jelly?

One

Eliason Harbor in Sitka looks like some genius dropped a trailer park at the edge of the Earth. All the shitty boats, gridded in their slips, like Laurel Lane laid overtop the water. The same barking dogs. The same old fuckers in greasy sweatpants waddling around mumbling. There's even a boat with a pink plastic flamingo tied to the rail. We had one of those. My mom loved the way it stuck out in the winter. When the sun hit it just right, the light smeared like lipstick across the snow. Every time some trailer kids stole it, she went out and got another one from the Dollar Tree. What does that say about her? Stubbornness, or particularity? Maybe they're the same thing. There's a lot of her in me. I keep flipping open my phone like maybe she'll be calling at that exact second. The dog-bit hand stops me from dialing. That's it, the hand. My fingers are swollen and fat like a baby's. It hurts a lot in a constant kind of way that's spreading up my wrist.

My mom used to say wish in one hand, shit in the other, see which one fills up first. Mr. Pritchard used to say your future likes to find you working, which I'm just now realizing is the exact same thing.

I ate all those pills on the ferry and now I'm guided by pain, pushing further and further down the dock. The harbor's different than Klak's. Small boats stacked high with filthy crab pots. Big rusting seiners piled with nets, heavy tugboats with bulldog faces, little aluminum charter boats with names like *Pole Dancer*, *The Hull Truth*, *The Aboat Time*, *The Aquaholic*. Rotting live-aboards everywhere—floating trailers—houseplants and old bicycles on deck. One has a wooden doghouse in the shape of a boat on the bow.

I am looking for one boat in particular.

Deckhands in orange raingear scrub salmon trollers. I walk the dock and watch them work. Tired, proud, strutting, white, Native, Hispanic, one strong Black woman sleeved with a bloody-fresh tattoo of a whale on her arm. I want them to nod at me, nod like the slime line workers in Klak. Some sort of secret club. Understanding, solidarity. What does that even mean? It was the word I was looking for when Sven and I argued on mushrooms. I'm seeing now that there were contracts in those nods. Contracts I broke. The most connected I've ever felt was mending nets next to Bonnie and sliming next to Bayram.

There's your lesson, learned too late.

On the outlying docks live the yachts, huge and blindingly white. There's a sunroom, a hot tub. Decks piled on decks. A crew member in a clean polo is scrubbing the gunwale with a squeegee on a long metal pole and docked behind the yacht, like a thorn or a toothache or a popup ad, is the *Ida U.*

I pass it and walk the docks and watch the tide run and listen to the wind rattling the trollers' riggings like low ugly wind chimes, and then I walk the harbor again, down each long creaking finger. Weather is coming and boats are coming in ahead of it, taking turns through the breakwater channel. Clouds tumble in, and past the mountains, at the horizon, the world's end, a skinny belt of sky is dripping with gold.

It takes me three passes before I stop and look at the boat. Let it move to the soft space behind my eyes. It's green, or used to be green, and boxy like a caboose. It's been a long time since it moved. There's a knocking on the door of my chest. A hard knock, like a cop. Talk radio is playing. The wind smells fresh. The boat bobs, and I think about how my own brain is floating inside of my skull. It's nice to have something in common. Like the moon. We're all seeing the same one. It's out now, in the evening, behind the boat. It's the color of pus. I know what's happening, why my eyes go up. The God of distraction. Look down. Look hard. The deck's piled high with ropes and boat parts. The top half of the Dutch door is open and the sleek black head of a dog pops up and cants sideways, looking back at me. Yellow eyes. One bent ear. A little white soul patch under his lips, like a middle school music teacher.

My dad had a dog? I sling my bag over my shoulder and walk away.

Two

I'm not ashamed about the festival. Once I started crying, I just couldn't stop. I spent a whole day on those steps, sobbing. People loved me for it. All the tutus took turns sitting by me, telling me about their bad mushroom trips. One guy said he shrunk down so small he could climb into his girlfriend's pussy and jump around, like a bounce house. This was how he learned to accept that he needed boner pills. Someone else opened a box with her own death inside. When I asked her what it looked like, she said she couldn't explain it.

I said, "Try."

She said, "It looks exactly like you'd expect it to."

I saw myself swimming.

The little girl with my blood in her hair brought me a bouquet of fireweed. I let her friends paint my face and even the free-range dogs came to see me. A big husky with a cloudy eye laid on my lap and tried to lick my palm. I think it was him. I think he was sorry.

Eventually I went back to my tent and laid in it and tried to will hate. Something to keep me moving forward. I thought about Sven and Jarrod and Kevin and myself. It sifted through me and was gone. Humiliation was all that was left. I walked out past the gate and down the long gravel road toward the highway, holding up my phone, looking for service. I had two new messages. I almost deleted them, thinking it was the cops again.

Bonnie's voice. She said, *Hey you son of a bitch. I dunno why I'm even doing this but I guess it's important because here I am. Does the name Ida U ring a fucking bell to you? It's a troller in Sitka. I had to go have a prayer with the God Squad just to get it. Fuck off and Good Luck. I mean it.*

Ida U, as in Ulma. Ida Ulma Deaver. He'd named it after my grandma.

The second: *It's me again Garrett. Also thought you oughta know I'm glad the motherfucker burned down. I'm glad it's done with. To the wind with all these sons-of-bitches!*

I called her back, left a voicemail saying it wasn't me, it was Jarrod. I left another thanking her for everything she'd done for me, and one more saying I'm glad she told me that story about Otis, glad that she thought I was worth telling. Then I hitched back to Anchorage and saw the Facebook message from Bayram. I told him there was a shipping problem on my end, some customs bullshit, and I wired him everything I made from herring and salmon, except for the cost of a ferry ticket and a hundredsomething in cash to keep me floating. Told him I managed to swing a good deal. It was like $4,300. Then I stopped answering his messages. It was the best idea I could come with at the time.

Sitka's a long way south, halfway to Vancouver, and everything here's still green. Downtown there's a hotel with a forty-foot totem pole near the front door. So many T-shirt shops and fur shops selling caribou fur lingerie and beaver hats. I walk past an Army recruitment office, stop, think about it, laugh at myself, keep walking. Past the Russian gift shop and past an ivory shop that says, "Authentic Native Scrimshaw on order." Six tourists walk by in matching blue fleeces. One of them has a life-size toy puffin under her arm.

There's a bar called Goldie's Goodtime Saloon where it's nice and dark. On the wall above the bar there's the top half of an enormous salmon combined with the back half of a deer. A plaque says: "Taken in the mountains of Sitka at great personal risk. 1967." The bartender's a worn, pretty woman with short black hair and a long face creased with deep smile lines. She has a broken front tooth and a straight nose. When I give her my ID she holds it to the light, studies it, then slides it back and walks through a swinging door into the kitchen. I wait. A white guy in a drug rug comes from behind the doors and points at me. "Thirsty?"

I get a beer from a tap with a plastic polar bear on the handle and then another. Drug Rug is telling some guy in a Hawaiian shirt about his new shotgun. A pump-action, pistol-grip, tactical home defense weapon that can supposedly shoot through door locks. There's something terrifying about hippies with guns—people that are super chill until, all at once, they're not. I wonder if he'd let me borrow it.

"Excuse me?" A gold bracelet is reaching toward me, a long thin hand attached to it, a long thin arm attached to the hand, attached to the bartender with the broken tooth. She's looking at me like there's a rash on my face.

She says, "I'm Jen. Your dad's Jen."

How long can I go without blinking?

"I was your father's girlfriend."

It feels like a really long time.

"Luke," she says to the Drug Rug. And again, louder. "Luke! This is Duane's son, Garrett." And practically everyone at the bar turns to me and looks.

Three

Count among my father's friends Drug Rug and an old fisherman who leads with the fact that he's nearly blind and a really fat guy with a black ponytail and a tattoo that says ASS on the back of his hand and a Tlingit guy with spiked hair and a baggy polyester Hawaiian print shirt. This is them. The boys. They take turns shaking my hand, like a receiving line. They all knew my father from the bar or the harbor, where many of them live on their boats. Goldie's has a coin-operated shower, ASS man says. It's the cleanest shower in town. That's why it's their favorite bar. That's why it was my dad's favorite bar. My father, they say, *appreciated* a clean shower.

They've all rallied around me and stand like a phalanx of bullies. Every time one steps closer the rest of them follow and somehow they're all talking at the same time, talking to/at/about me. What's wrong with my hand? They wanted to send me a card. Rug was supposed to buy it. No, Shirt. No, Jen. Have I seen much of Alaska? No, it doesn't matter who was supposed to buy the card but the point is that they had wanted to send a condolence along with an invitation to visit. Really, is that hand okay?

I tell them it is.

I get the basic facts of Sitka.

Next week's weather forecast.

More people I should meet.

Sad eyes all staring at me.

"And you really do look like him."

"Right down to the hairline. A dead ringer!"

"Don't you get any ideas, Jen!"

"How are you holding up?"

"What a terrible tragedy."

"What a freak accident."

"What?"

"What?"

"What?"

"How long are you staying again?"

I'm sweating and cold, just like this polar bear beer.

"What did you just say?" It was the guy in the Aloha print. There's a neon Miller Lite sign behind my head, and I can see the blue light reflected in his glasses. His face says surprise.

"Sorry," I say. "What about the accident?"

"Let's give him a little breathing room," Jen says. "I'm sure he's exhausted."

ASS asks, "Why didn't you tell us the kid was coming? I would've taken off work."

I'm trying to talk but Jen covers for me. "Because I knew you guys would act like this."

Rug says, "We can still take him up Flat Top Mountain!"

Another polar bear beer is placed into my hand. It's Jen. She says, "Just keep drinking until they make sense."

"Excuse me," I say. "It was a long flight from Pittsburgh."

In the bathroom the showers are a dollar but the solitude is free. I close and lock the door and slap myself in the face and tie my shoes in case I gotta run. One side of my face is welted now and in the sink the water circles the drain, traces of him maybe still down there. His hair, his skin. Tangled up with all the other rotting parts of men, a garbage patch crawling toward the sea. I make myself noodle-thin and follow him down. Through wedding rings, past needling fields of stubble, rusting pipes, soap, pus, and a whole new kind of slime. One time I threw up at a wad of my hair my mother pulled from the shower grate, and look at me now. Duane, down the drain. I'm in pain. More of the same.

Ha!

Wait.

You're standing in a bathroom in a bar in Sitka, Alaska.

Pritchard: Your brain is a muscle and, Garrett, you need to flex it.

Flex: Would it change your mind if I told you your father killed himself?

What a weird way to put it, especially for a guy who always says he's no good with words. Why lie? And now, the floor. It's cold and not as clean as advertised. Dirt grinding into my palms, and did I just sit, or did I collapse? Action, or accident? Accidents just don't carry the same type of *why*. Get real, Beaver:

You need the why. The momentum of the why. The focus and the meaning in it and now someone knocking on the door. Gentle this time. Jen. I wash my face, check my hand. The cotton balls are turning yellow.

Why—

They want to know if I'm hungry. Have I seen the town? It's the totem pole capital of the world. Shirt's cousin Ben Samuel is a master carver. He even erected a shame pole directed at George W. Bush. Not to get political; your father had no politics to speak of—

"Not true," Jen says. "He just didn't announce them."

"If I had to guess," ASS says, "he was on the side of individual freedom."

"Nevertheless," Rug says, "he was a very helpful man."

"He was a *real* ladies' man," ASS says.

"And a real man's man," Rug says.

"A friendly guy," Shirt says.

"He had hands, though," ASS man says.

"Your father," the blind one says, "he helped me get home when I was too puckered to walk a few different times."

"And how many times did he steal your wallet?" Jen says.

They all break up laughing, deep like maniacs and I start laughing too, louder and harder than the rest of them. I slap my knee. "One time," I say, "he scooped up a roadkill deer, tied it to a tree, and drove his truck into it to get the insurance money."

Glorious humor.

I stand from the barstool and say, "Then he left my mom and me and never came back."

I watch them shuffle and step back. Their eyes hitting the floor, hands looking for someplace better to be—pockets, shirt buttons, hats to be adjusted, phones to be flipped, drinks that need lifting. It makes me feel better. Powerful.

"You guys know about barratry, right?"

"We can tell bar stories later," Jen tells them. "Garrett and I have a few things to do." They're sad to see me go. They pat me and bow their stupid heads.

"Ready?" she says, guiding me out of the door.

It's pissing rain and we walk through it with our hoods up. Jen asks what I thought about the boat and I say I literally just got to town. She takes my bag from me and puts it on her shoulder.

"I looked out the window this morning and swore I saw your father's ghost."

She stops and turns. We're under a streetlight in front of a tourist lodge, the one with the totem pole. All the mountains are gone now, killed by the rain. There's a big, covered porch looking out over the water and a bunch of touristy guys are smoking cigars on it. It smells like a book on fire. Jen's looking down at my XTRATUFs. She says nice boots. She says they look broken in already.

I say, "I thought he killed himself."

My bag hits the ground. An old beater truck with one headlight passes. I'm blind, and when I can see again, Jen's still there, saying "Is that what your mother said? I told her *undetermined* when I called for your address. Un-*fucking*-determined. I said it was a *possibility*. I had to talk on the phone with these fucking cops in Hawaii like six times before they ruled it an accident."

And it makes a strange type of sense. I can see them on the phone together. The long-distance static. My mom pacing, Flex in the living room, pants unbuttoned, mouth-breathing, the TV turned down so he can listen in. And later, after the call, my mother's saying Poor Garrett. She's telling Flex about how when I was a kid I'd stand at the end of the hallway and howl and then cry when my own echo howled back. She's saying everyone needs a clean break.

Jen's saying, "They kept asking if he showed any signs of distress."

She's saying, "He fished for a living. Of course he was fucking distressed."

She's saying, "It was all just some liability bullshit with the hotel."

She's saying, "I tried to keep your mother updated but she stopped returning my calls."

She's saying, "I'm so sorry you're only just hearing this now."

She's saying, "I wish you'd called me. I left her my number."

She's saying, "Let's keep walking. It's cold."

Four

The harbor, the gangway, the docks—there's something so sad and so funny and so right about living on the water and dying on the concrete. Running off to the cold, then dying in the heat. I'm not saying that's what he deserved. But I am happy his boat's a piece of shit.

"Beaver," Jen says, stepping over the rail onto the wet deck. "Beaver, somebody's coming to see you." The dog shoots up from the Dutch door, whining.

"The dog's named Beaver?"

"Your dad thought it was hilarious, naming something after something different. He used to have a cat named Fish."

"I get it."

"Most of the time, he just called the dog Junior."

Quiet.

"I probably shouldn't have said that."

I say it's fine. Fine is such a funny word because it never means what it actually means. The boat pitches a little when I step on deck, not enough to make my stomach drop but still my stomach drops, and when Jen opens the door the dog tries to climb me like there's a good view from the top of my head. He's all ribs, a xylophone with fur. When I pet him, he cries for more. I get that impulse now. Can he smell my father in my sweat? Is he mistaking pheromones for memories?

I get that now, too.

Jen says my dad bought him to guard the boat and go out on fishing trips but he welcomes everyone like the Pope. She's funny. Why does she have to be funny? I duck and follow her into the cabin. It's the size of a small bedroom, the walls lined with ugly plywood cupboards. Everything's so neat and compact, a place for everything but the stack of books she moves from a milkcrate to the floor. I ask if my dad was a reader and she says the only book she ever saw him open was a checkbook.

She slides me the crate, says sit.

Now she's sitting and there's a bowl of chips between us. Doritos, the Cool Ranch kind. Blue speckles. She's different from my mom in almost every way. I ask her if she's ever wondered why they're called Cool Ranch. Like, what makes them cool? She hasn't wondered. She says I didn't come here to talk about chips.

"I'm sorry to start off like this," she says. "I can't imagine what it's like, thinking one thing, then learning another."

"It's alright," I say. "It doesn't really matter in the grand scheme of things."

She scoffs, says, "Maybe she was just confused about what I said. I really wanted to send you some of his things. But when she ignored my calls, I figured that was the end of it."

"She wasn't confused."

"She seemed lovely on the phone. She asked me my birthday."

"Numerology," I tell her. "She thinks numbers have all the answers."

She says, "Is she an economist?" and drumrolls the table with her fingers.

"Well," she says. "This is fun!"

She stuffs her face with chips. Whole handfuls at once, turning the corners to fit them into her mouth with the dog scavenging for crumbs below our feet. She says through a mouthful that she eats when she's nervous. I tell her when I get nervous I usually just have to go to the bathroom, so we better get into it.

She says, "I met your father maybe ten years ago when he signed on as my dad's deckhand. He was a *really* good deckhand. Most the guys that make good deckhands save up and buy some piece of shit boat and work it a few years and when they break even, they sell it and buy a better boat. By the time they're my dad's age they've got everything paid for, and hopefully they can sell the boat and retire. Duane thought he needed a boat, too. Or we did. We got serious fast. What can I say? He had a way with words. And it had to be a wooden boat. He was romantic that way. *Fiberglass just doesn't have a heart.*"

She sticks her finger in her mouth in a Gag Me sort of motion.

"Then he bought this fucking dud." She knocks on the wall. "He put some money into it and we fished it together for a couple of years. But you spend seven, eight days out there together and everything gets so goddamned personal. I grew up fishing the Cape and so I know a lot. He hated that. People from outside are always like that. They make up for not being Alaskan by being *extra Alaskan.*

"One time, we were fishing winter kings in thick fog, so thick you could chew it, and he missed spotting a boat on the port side and we passed so close our poles banged together and all the rigging got bound up. We spent two hours bobbing in the water just to get everything unfucked. It cost us maybe three grand. Duane blamed me, but it was his fucking fault, and I said he could either have a girlfriend or a deckhand but I sure as hell wouldn't be both. I went back to bartending and he had like five good seasons. But he was awful with the little things. Fishing's mostly minutia—you get the permits, change the oil, buy the dry goods, rig the gear, sign logs, load up with ice. He had no patience for any of it. He hated the regulations. Hated the prices they gave him at the processor, but he wouldn't join the co-op. Said it tied him down. Typical libertarian shit."

She stands and spins the lid off a bucket of dog food by the captain's chair and scoops some into a metal bowl. "I wonder what the motherfucking chef is cooking up for you?" she says to the dog.

"'I wonder what the motherfucking chef is cooking up for you?' That's what your dad always said to him. He was such a boy. Easy to dote on, hard to love. Am I talking a lot? I talk a lot when I'm nervous, too."

I say, "No." Out the cabin window the sun's fading and the light looks grainy like an old picture. We watch the blue thicken and she flicks her cigarette into the seashell on the table.

"You want me to empty your ashtray?"

She laughs, says, "Nope. When they're full, I pitch the shell in the water and find another one on the beach. Believe it or not, it was your father's idea. He said I'd smoke less and walk more. He had a theory about everything."

The night moves on, and she tells me stories. About her dad and the fisherman's co-op he started way back in the 1970s, and her mom, from a little village on the other side of the island. And stories about my dad and his bar buddies and all the stupid shit they did, and I'm hearing her and seeing the things around me and it feels like zooming in on something far away. Like I'm double-clicking until part of an image gets bigger. Bigger, not clearer. Blurry still. Maybe it can't be sharpened. Until, somewhere in the pixels, finally, I see what I want to know.

"Did he talk about me very much?"

"Fuck," she says.

I watch her look past me, out one window then the other, and I already know what comes next. She says, "Garrett, I never even knew you existed. You or your mother. The coroner in Hawaii asked me if I wanted to contact you, and I was like, contact who? I still don't know how they knew that. Your dad always said he was against marriage *philosophically*, whatever that means. He said he didn't want kids. It's been a wild few months. It's been really..."

"Humiliating."

"Yep," she says. "It gets so easy to start wondering what else is made up, you know?"

"Like everybody's in on the joke but you."

"I guess we're in the same boat."

"Captain, we're sinking!"

She laughs, knocks on the wooden table, says it's getting late. She says I should stay on the boat. She's been staying at her dad's anyway.

"Do you know what magnetite is?" I ask her as she's packing a bag down in the cuddy. "The stuff in salmon that directs them."

She peeks through the plaid curtain. Grinning.

I say, "That's how I feel. Just like a salmon. Like I keep getting pulled to some spot I can't even ever remember being. Like it's genetic."

The smile is getting wider.

"What's so funny?"

She says, "My mother was Tlingit." She grabs a strand of her hair, black, and she waves it at me. "I'm Tlingit. Men make such a big thing about it. Did I know how to salt fish? Did I have elders? Most those guys wanted a little fishwife. But your dad was never like that, and when I met him, I thought he was just intimidated. I really knew so much more about this life than he did. But when he fell, and I found out about you and your mother, it finally clicked. That man just didn't believe in the past. Or history, or identity, anything. I swear it was like the more he thought about mine, the more he'd have to reckon with his own. He actually told me that his parents were both dead."

"His father is," I say. "Suicide."

She nods.

"My point is my whole life I've been hearing white people tell me how they're like a salmon or whatever. You're not a fucking fish. If you were, you'd be heading back to Pennsylvania by now. You see what I mean?"

And I don't, not really, but I want to—for myself, and for her.

She comes up from the cuddy and hands me the keys to the door. She says, "You're in a bad way aren't you?"

I tell her I am. I tell her I was at a processor but now I'm broke. She says I should stick around and meet her dad when he comes in from fishing. She says the boys are still at the bar if I want to go. They'll buy me drinks.

"Thanks," I say. "But I never want to see those fucking people ever again."

Five

I lay in the berth in my dad's boat watching the hours tick by and soon it's 4:45, 8:45 in Pennsylvania, and I walk up to the lot above the harbor and sit on a bench next to the cinderblock bathrooms and trace the numbers on the keypad with my swollen thumb. A grown-ass man in a Minnesota Timberwolves jersey is circling the lot on a kids' BMX bike, eyeing me. The jersey number's eleven, my mom's favorite. It's a powerful number, eleven. Essential. Symmetrical. On its side, an equal sign. She has them all memorized, the powerful numbers, but supposedly I'm the OCD one.

One time, after I'd gotten into a fight in the sixth grade, my mom bought a 2XL Nike hoodie from the Goodwill and cut the Swoosh and the letters from it while she sat cross-legged on the couch watching her shows. She sat a lot like Bonnie, making herself small, trying to sew herself into her work. She sewed it onto a fresh K-Mart hoodie. She even cut the tag from the inside. We were always so fucking broke! When I put it on, I boiled with embarrassment. Not because we didn't have any money, because she thought we could pretend. I know it must be hurtful, me running off to Alaska. She probably thinks that's why I did it.

No shit—

"Andersons." She answers the phone like Flex now. All business.

"Mom," I say. "Hey." In the twilight I see the little blue islands, way out. Past them, the horizon's soft edge. I'd like to describe it to her, but there's no way to make it real.

"My God!" she says. I haven't heard that tone in her in forever. The pep of it. "I was just telling Flex if you didn't call your mother soon, I might just have to track you down. Where are you?"

"Alaska," I say.

"Alaska," she says. "If I had a dime every time I heard that! I've been needing to tell you something."

"Listen, mom. I know that . . ."

"Flex and I are having a baby. A little girl."

"Like from your body?"

She says, "We've been trying, but I thought we were shit out of luck. I'm forty-four, Garrett! But I knew it had to be two evens, for balance. And for a second kid!"

There's a sea lion in the harbor, rolling in an empty slip under the dock light. Water cascading off his back and a few early morning tourists taking pictures. This whole time I'd been thinking my mom was hiding news about my dad *for* me. But it was for her. She was trying to make something brand new and there I was tugging at the past. There's a joy there without me, I can feel it coming through the phone. A life I'm not a part of, and, the way I see it, I can either be a zit or an asterisk on that life. I used to think I was a zit. Like I was getting picked at. Like I'd scab over and heal if everyone would just leave me alone. I was wrong. I usually am. I tell her congratulations. I tell her I also have big news. Deaver the Beaver has joined the Marines.

I say, "Did you hear me?"

"Oh Garrett. Are you sure that's what you want?"

It's her surprise that chokes me up. The slack in her voice almost makes me backslide, say Gotcha, I'm sinking here. I swallow it, tell her it's a done deal, shipping out from Alaska tomorrow, and you can throw out my stuff in the basement, and yep, I'll send you an address, and yep, I'm telling the truth, yep, I passed the physical, the psych, too, and when the phone snaps shut, it feels like closing a heavy book I know I'll never finish. Like I don't have the vocab I need to finish it.

Six

Jen says three days until her dad gets in from fishing and maybe then he'll have some work for me. Until then, accelerol makes the yellow angel eyes look away. Accelerol makes my hand stop hurting. So does meth. Just once. Well, thrice. I'm not proud. I'm not ashamed either. I just *am*. That shit tastes like a dryer sheet on fire. It smells like batteries. In an alley behind the worst bar in town with two guys I just met and one of them is in a Timberwolves Jersey. Four sets of eyes blinking at the human leg I found. They say no shit, man. Wild.

Wild—

With a finger snap its morning in Sitka and the sun's bright and there's snow on the mountains, postcard shit, and I'm walking down Main Street shivering, having just woken up in a bush behind the library, heading toward the harbor, to my dad's boat. I just couldn't sleep there.

Sometimes you can make a lie true. You can make a bed and lie in it. Pritchard called it manifesting. At the Tesoro I manifest some accelerol into my pocket. The clerk is eyeing me. In the bathroom I wash the ugly weak salt from my cheeks and then I manifest a bag of gummy worms and ignore the clerk hollering at me out the door. There's a cruise ship the size of God anchored in the bay, ferrying in tourists, crowding the sidewalks, lost, rubbernecked, huge cameras, loose purses, super stealable, and I'm thinking about trying to lift one when I hear the two words I hate most.

"Garrett Deaver?"

The school colors come first—navy and white, the collegiate font on the chest, G STATE, then the square jaw, the two-day stubble, the Young Republican haircut, parted just right. Behind him, maybe a brother, a flannel over a hoodie, backwards hat, and two perfect parents trailing, carrying shopping bags from the fur outlet.

"Mike?" I say. "Miller Hall?"

"No, fucker. Derek."

He grabs his brother, says he can't fucking believe it but right here's the psycho that upper-decked his girlfriend's apartment.

I say, "You have been manifested."

"We couldn't figure it out for two days!"

"Every time we flushed it, it got worse!"

"We had to pay a plumber!"

And now they're getting closer.

I say, "You sure you're not Mike?"

And I'm backed up against the wall of the Russian gift shop.

"Look at you," he's saying. "What the fuck happened to you?" And now they're pushing me, poking, and all the tourists are passing us, thinking this is normal, this is Alaska, and

there is no far enough away, that's clear to me now, and I scream
BEAR, and point, and my knee finds Derek's nuts, and I'm
running down the street with the brother chasing me, and
they're fast, they probably play lacrosse, and I cut through an
alley off of Main Street, and stop at the storefront where the
people in the posters got those stern faces. Serious eyes, Holly-
wood jaws. Helmets. Life's tough, get a helmet. Pritchard used
to say that.

"Hey!" The brothers are coming.

When I open the door, the recruiter stands from a desk
covered in tchotchkes. He's pale and paunchy and buzz-cut.
He looks like he's the physical representation of his job. Like he
has become his work. Someday he'll wake up to find that he's
actually a swivel chair. His feet might be turning into castors
right now. His name might be Sergeant Swivel. He's talking to
me but I'm missing words. It might be the fever.

"Hello!" I say to him. "It's nice to see you again."

"Have we met?" He has an American flag pin on his tie.
"Take a seat."

I sit or maybe collapse. There are posters everywhere. More
big stern faces. Flags. Guns. I remember holding Bonnie's wok in
my hand. Skulking through the alders at night. The coffee mug
against Jarrod's head. The supreme joy of the righteous.

I say, "I think we met earlier in the summer. Earlier in the
summer at that party."

Sergeant Swivel spins a pencil in his hand. "Is that so?
You mean at Jim's barbecue? What's your name, again? You a
friend of Jim?"

I say, "I don't blame you for forgetting. You were drinking very heavily. Binge-drinking, some might say." He's giving me a really concerned look. A single drop of sweat grazes my ear and I shake with the willies. "I think you drove home. Everyone was laughing at you. Anyway, my name is Garrett, and I am twenty-two years old and I would like to help the children."

He looks past me and I follow his eyes. Outside the brothers are peering in the window.

Swivel tells me that I've come to the right place because there are plenty of opportunities for me to help the children, at home and abroad, and when I tell him that I have a bachelor's degree in psychology, he says that he has tremendous—tremendous—respect for young men, and *increasingly* women, who decide to serve *after* receiving some higher education. He asks if I would like a beverage and I ask if he has any meth and/or alcohol and he says Funny Guy! And points two fingers at me.

"Water would be tremendous," I tell him. "There are two competing teams of sweat bobsledding down my ass crack."

He asks what's going on with my hand and I tell him that a dog bit me when I was on drugs. Behind him a portrait of George W. Bush smiles at me. Those ears. That grin. I remember Pritchard pouting the day they hung the new Bush portrait on the school office wall. I remember that Pritchard had a fresh haircut. Swivel has a fresh haircut. Both of them and their paunches, their sad chipboard desks. What's up with the hair? Pritchard says he's quitting. He says he's going to work at a bank two days a week and help his brother run their family farm. I ask if we can keep meeting and he fumbles his words, trying to say No.

Now, with both of them talking, I can't make out much. But I know the big idea is pride. They both think I've made good choices. They think I have bright futures. They believe in service to the common good. Whose sacrifice? Whose good? They're brothers, I see that now. I want to know why they didn't tell me sooner.

Swivel says, "Tell you what?"

"Why are you quitting?"

Swivel says, "I'm going to get a second recruiter to sit in with us."

Pritchard says, "This job is destroying my mental health."

Now Kevin is behind him, patting my dad on the back.

They want me to sit down and try to relax. Please. Their voices are in harmony. Who do these assholes mistake me for? Who put Swivel's letter opener in my palm? Who loaded the family gun for me, again? Oh, Garrett, you're fucked now. Those little blue islands, way out, just swim! Swivel is standing at the threshold with two bottles of water. He wants me to set the letter opener down. He wants it out of my hands and now it tastes brassy in my mouth. At the end of the handle is the head of a bear with little jewels for eyes. Winking at me.

"Please."

It's not even very sharp. Sharp enough, with a running start. The wall. The magnetic pull of it. I'm ready, I'm swimming, and the chair takes me out at the knees. Swivel's behind his desk now. A paperweight flies at me and hits the wall. The fear of me on his face is embarrassing. We should all be so embarrassed. He's coming for me now. His hands are on my coat. He's got me by my coat. I say get away from me you guy and then he has an empty coat. He's laying on the floor, small now, or maybe I've grown. Maybe I punched him in the face. A bell jingles crazily when I throw open the door. Swivel is yelling at me to stop. But nothing can stop me. Zooooom—past the church, interrupting Derek's family taking a photo. Past the fur bikini storefront, past Goldie's and through the sound of the laughing men spilling out from the open bar door.

I cut through the alley by an antique store and pop into the little souvenir shop across from the McDonald's. It's empty and so I buy a hoodie that says GUT FISH?! and a fake-fur bomber hat. That'll be fifty dollars, the woman says. She has a tube piping oxygen into her nose. I give her my last three twenties and don't wait for the change.

Outside in my new bear shirt and I cut through a neighborhood, walking slow, stopping to look out at the water. The cruise ship's so big it makes the mountains look small. A tourist passes me, says, "Some ship, ain't it?"

"Vello," I say. "Vow are you?"

"Enjoy America!" he says. He keeps walking.

I don't feel so great.

Sirens. They're far off.

Now they're closer.

To the wind—

At the processors along cannery row, the workers are changing shifts. They're walking down the road with their lunch bags slung over their shoulders, walking slow, one of them riding that stolen bike with another guy standing on the pegs. He yells at me, "It is too late. She loves another." And they laugh. Another one yells, "The boat left yesterday," and they slap their knees laughing.

Someone yells. "Just piss in the bushes."

"You have outrun the bear."

"What have you stolen?"

Haha, Motherfuckers.

Hahahahahahaha

Hahahahahaha

Hahahahaha

Hahahaha

Hahaha

Haha

Ha

Sirens and cold sweat. At the harbor, I let the panting stop. I toss the hoodie and hat in the trash and walk down the dock, past the trollers getting zipped up for the season. Four Native kids are painting a big blue seiner called "Big Blue." When I pass, the wind tosses a drop of oil paint from one kid's brush and it slaps me in the forehead where my third eye should be. Nice weather. Beautiful day. How's the fishing? I smile and nod. I chit and chat. I play it cool. Cool as a cat, man, purr. I wink or maybe just twitch. It's afternoon and the docks are busy. The charter captains are cutting up their catch for the tourists taking pictures. Big dark cohos. Rockfish the color of traffic cones. The clementines Bay gave me! What do you do when even your guilt feels selfish?

By the time I make it to the *Ida U*, I can see a cop car circling the lot above the harbor. It stays and stays. I change my
clothes and shave my face and head and toss the hair out the
window and watch it float. There's this toothache pain leaking
out of my hand. I take some aspirin, some accelerol. I smoke the
tiny butt of a cigarette Jen left in the seashell and then another. I
down the tequila in the mini-fridge freezer.

The car is still there.

I'm certain it's real.

I draw all the blinds tight, kill the cabin lights.

Seven

I peek through the blinds and the car's still there.

I look again and it's gone.

I lay in the berth and see my mom's face when she finds out I'm in jail. There's nothing smug about it. That's the worst part. No lifted eyebrow, no chin tilted up. The weight of it tugs on her cheeks. She's at the kitchen table. Flex is behind her, fat hands on her shoulders. He swallows the told-you-so's until he turns pink.

When I think of my mom now, I always end up thinking about Bonnie. I took psych. I remember that Jung shit. This one day, Bonnie and I were working in her shack and she asked me to hand her a spool of line. I asked her about the difference between *line* and *rope* and she said something about how rope was just unemployed line. But the second a rope gets a purpose—tied to a shit bucket or used to hoist a stabilizer or woven into a net—it becomes line. It helps to know the difference so you can leave a working line alone.

"For example," she said. "If you hung yourself on a boat, the rope would be line."

I said, "Gotcha," and we both shut up.

There was so much pain in her I never even considered.

The cop car comes and goes. I keep the lights off and stay in the cuddy and laugh at myself and laugh on top of those laughs. Get this—there are no roads out of Sitka, literally none. I have a few bloody ones balled in my back pocket. That's it. It's starting to get dark, low clouds over the mountains. Two cops on the lip of the gangway talking with the harbormaster in his orange vest. They're pointing down toward our finger of the dock. I strip off my clothes and pack them into my bag and jam the bag deep into the cuddy, and after they descend the ramp and disappear behind the trollers in the slips between us, I leave the cabin and sneak around to the portside rail facing the sea. It's already cold. My hair's standing on end. Even my balls know what's coming.

The cops are talking with a woman on the little catamaran a few slips down. When I hear her say *green F/V*, I drop into the water. Breathless cold, so cold it's hot, and I can't recover before a wake from a boat motoring through the breakwater pushes me against the hull and my head hits the side. I push off, hit it again. This time I stick. I'm stuck, waiting. The waves die and my jaw's quaking already, fucking fluttering, and I peek around the bow just as the cops pass. It's dark. The water's black. It stinks like fuel and I'm dizzy and Bonnie told me they find guys face-down in harbors all the time, too drunk or high to climb back onto the dock. That's me. That's what the tox screen will say. Maybe they'll call it suicide. My mom will shake her head.

Blub.

I grab a deep breath, push off the bow, enter.

Inside of it now, the black. Fumbling naked, scorched lungs, reaching out and kicking. There's light stabbing the water and I go deeper and I kick through my stinging eyes and just when I think I can't go any more, my hand finds the metal of a piling. I follow it up, the slats of light, the gross air under the dock. They're right above me. I can hear them talking. The harbormaster's saying they can go back and contact the boat owner.

"Well," he says. "The owner's old lady. Owner's dead."

The cop says, "We'll send a car around the lot."

"Was this some sort of anti-war thing?"

"Maybe," he says. "Or just another fucking tweaker."

I'm eating holes in my lips so they can't hear me shivering. The tide's running out and taking me with it, tugging on my legs. There's no point in waiting, in thinking, I just swim like a motherfucker until I come up against this big, refurbished tugboat that tourists pay to sleep on. I pop up and gulp for air and hear voices from the deck.

"Is it the sea lion again?"

"Get the camera."

A light swoops toward me and I'm gone. The burning in my chest, and if this is freedom maybe I'll take jail, if this is living maybe I'll take death, take anything warm and full of air and I'm up again but I don't know where. It's getting really cold. I swim again, breathe, swim again. It hits me that even if I make it to a quiet part of the docks I might be too tired to climb back up.

"Is that somebody in the water?"

"Hey! Hey!"

Voosh—past the mainframe and Big Blue and toward an empty finger of the dock, the one with the broken lights, where maybe I can climb up and escape. Just a little further, just one more channel, the one by the breakwater, and Oh No, the wake of a boat entering the marina.

The low, choked engine, gurgling—

Dive.

Or maybe rise.

The hull scrapes my back and I'm drinking. My dad brought home a waterbed and when he was gone one night, I climbed into it and dreamed I was a fish. It's the same feeling now, deep down, falling through the water. Down to the sidewalk. Down to the place where the horizon dies, the line between choice. It wasn't ever as simple as jumping or falling. It's so clear from inside the moaning, down in the lungs that make pain. Who told me there'll be faces? There are none, nothing but the deep blue light, glowing like a phone call in the dark. Don't answer it. Let it ring.

Noise.

The air tears open. There's a life ring. I'm supposed to grab it. It's up, to the left, it's too high, high as heaven. The rudder's bubbling all around, and through the bubbles a dog barks. It's Beaver. He is my son. There's so much more left for me to unfuck! Down, again, but this time somebody says choose water. Stop fighting. Accept the line tangled around my legs.

But I see the myths that this would make of me, the way my story would crawl from the dead skin of lies, and I raise my dirty hand. I have it. I'm holding on and they're dragging me in. The blur of a Hawaiian shirt on the dock. They know my name. I try to say I'm fine. I'm okay.

And I am, until the festival dog comes back to bite me again.

—Down.

Eight

Knocking, and a dog barks. Pure blue above me and I'm in a field. The one behind the trailer, or the soccer field at G State where I used to like to sit and pretend to read and watch everyone else sitting in circles with their shoes left at the edges of blankets.

I'm in the cuddy of a boat. Not my dad's boat. Daylight through the escape hatch and a raven on the glass. The black dinosaur feet and the talons clicking. The curtain over the cuddy stairs closes. Someone whispers, "Shhh!" between his teeth.

"He don't bite," the voice says, a minute later. "What's missing now?"

"I came down to ask you about your deckhand. Had a kid get into some bullshit downtown then damn near got his head chopped off swimming in the marina. We think he was hiding out on the *Ida U*."

"It's always something, isn't it?" the voice says. "What'd he do?"

"Got into a scuffle with an army recruiter. Maybe a protest or something."

"Guy get hurt?"

"Nope."

"Well, that's good," the voice says. "But my deckhand went back to school yesterday morning. Took him to the airport myself."

"And you haven't had anybody staying on the *Ida U*?"

"Yeah, he was. The deckhand. But like I said, he went back to school. You want a coffee or something? I make the good stuff."

"No, I'm fine." I can hear their feet shuffling on the deck. I pull the sleeping bag over my face. The cabin door must be open because of how loud they are.

"You can't find a good deckhand anymore to save your fucking life. Jen did tell me there was a lot of stuff moved around on the deck over there."

"And you didn't bother to call us?"

"It's a harbor. If I called the cops every time something was shady, I'd never get anything done and neither would you. I'm just getting ready to head out and I'd like to do it before Jen comes down here and tells me I shouldn't be fishing alone."

"Well, good luck with it."

The cabin door closes and I can hear someone clearing the deck. I think I went down through the concrete and came out the other side. It would've been so easy down there, just to take a deep breath, fill up with water, let go. I think I wanted to. I think I tried. It was my dad's friend Shirt that jumped in and grabbed me and passed me off to Drug Rug. He slapped my back like a baby. I puked up some water and told them the cops were looking for me. They didn't even talk about it, didn't ask me a thing. They just took me down to some boat and put me in the berth to warm up. Whoever my dad was, those guys loved him.

Now the engine fires up and shakes the cuddy. The curtain snaps open. An old man's staring at me. He's small and crooked, with a face like a barn and dirty silver hair poking out from a hat that says GUT FISH?!

"Jesus, they were right," he says. "You look just like him."

"Where am I?"

"I'm Clem. Do you need to go to the hospital?"

"You didn't have to do that for me," I tell him.

"Get up. Check your ribs and shit. Can you breathe?"

"I'm good," I say, and I slide out of the berth.

"Come here," he says. He comes down into the cuddy and turns me around and presses his cold ear to my back. "Cough."

I cough.

"Man," he says. "You're all bruised up."

Some of it's leftover from Jarrod, but I don't bother. He says to stay below deck until we're out on the water or he's gonna leave me on a rock that covers at high tide.

"Where are we going?"

He says, "They got your boots from the *Ida U*. I pitched your trucker pills."

COLD WATER IMMERSION SUIT
FITS 59–72 INCHES
110–205 Pounds
Inspected 6/14/2006

DON SUIT ONLY WHEN CAPSIZE IS IMMINENT

INSTRUCTIONS:

1. IF TIME PERMITS REMOVE SHOES.
2. INSERT LEGS AND TIGHTEN ANKLE STRAPS.
3. PUT NON-DOMINANT ARM IN, THEN THE HOOD, THEN THE OTHER ARM.
4. PULL ZIPPER UP, TAKING CARE THAT CLOTHING IS NOT CAUGHT IN ZIPPER.
5. PULL CORD TO INFLATE RING AFTER ENTRY INTO WATER. EMERGENCY LIGHTS SHOULD BEGIN FLASHING WHEN RING IS INFLATED.
6. RELEASE FLARES IMMEDIATELY. SEA DYE SHOULD RELEASE AUTOMATICALLY.
7. RELAX! YOU CANNOT SINK!

Nine

It's 6 a.m., damp and cold on the deck of a forty-six-foot troller called the *Norma Dawn*, the sky and the sea the same gray, sun somewhere up there, or maybe over there, wherever, it's more of a concept than a real thing right now. This fog. It's a lot. It's solid. It swallowed us whole and there's salt on my lips and the waves are pounding the hull and suddenly, so suddenly, the seasickness grabs onto my insides and squeezes.

I tell Jen's dad I think I might puke.

"Good," he says. "Get all that poison out of you."

He decided to take me out fishing. He said he needed a deckhand and I needed to dry out and get out of Sitka for a few days. He didn't exactly give me a choice.

Clem—like something pulled from the sea, and he looks that way, too. Like a crustacean, straight-up barnicular, something that lives in salt, hugging rocks. Last night, at anchor outside of the Sitka, he explained how it works: you use a mechanical pulley, a *gurdy*, to drop a weighted cable a couple hundred feet deep, and you hook some smaller lines to that cable, and on those smaller lines you hook some lures, and when the boat moves forward—*trolls*—the lures get pulled through the water. When enough of the lures are full of fish you bring the cable up. You do this from the troll pit, a three-foot-deep recess in the back of the boat. If there's a fish on the line, you lean over the rail, hook it with a gaff, pull it in, bleed it, gill it, gut it, wash it, ice it.

Last night it sounded easy enough, especially after he gave me some old antibiotics from his stash for my hand. But now I'm down in the troll pit and Clem's next to me, teaching me how to use the gurdy to drop the line into the water. It squeals like the baby rabbits we used to catch in the trailer park. I drop my first line, watch the ocean take it.

Clem says, "That's the gist of it," and that's when the puking starts.

"Try and look at the horizon," he says. "It's the only thing that helps."

What horizon? The sea looks like liquid smoke. Or liquid glass. Or maybe mercury. Every time the light changes it feels new. The sea rocks one way and the boat rocks the other and bile, now. Yellow acid. I try to focus on the white cliffs, far off, miles away. Doesn't help.

"Best detox I know!" Clem says. "Now go get the knife sharpener."

I climb from the pit, stumble across the deck, and from the cabin, looking out the window, I can see the ocean buckle and heave in every direction. It's like we shrunk down overnight, like a tiny, compressed file lost somewhere. I stop to puke and lay for a minute on the deck. At least I know now I don't want to die.

When I get back to the troll pit, there're five fish in the slaughter bin.

I ask, "Is this normal?"

"It's not very nice out."

"I mean the puking."

"I don't know. It's not my body."

I gag.

I puke.

I puke again.

Sounds like a dog puking.

And now it's slimy and green, laced with black.

"Bite's on," Clem says. "Untuck your pecker."

We run the lines. Clem can swing a coho into the boat without using the gaff. He just pulls the line and they fly into the slaughter bin. When I try, the fish flies off the line and back into the water. He docks five bucks from my pay. It's whatever. My lines are full. King, king, coho, coho, king. Case of beer for a king. Cup of coffee for a coho. That's how he explained my pay. After an hour, that's what I start to see. I gaff a case of beer in the head and the eye pops out. I dig my pointer finger into the gills of a coffee cup and rip. Blood drains from the cup. The tail slaps the slaughter bin, splatters. When the flopping stops I hook the gills in my pointer finger and saw them out with the knife tip— the soft, fine filaments, like eyelashes dipped in blood. Puke. I slit the white belly. The soft hiss of gas escaping. The egg skein tears. Little pink balls all over the slaughter bin. Everything comes out clean except for the heart. I cut it out. Dime-sized. Purple. It beats fourteen times on the edge of my knife.

The will to live, and all that.

"You can't dick around when the bite's on," Clem says.

I scrape the blood from the veins of the coffee cup. Clean the kidney line of the beer. Rinse the blood and slime. Drop eleven cups of coffee and seven cases of beer down the chute into the fish hold. I run the lines, catch a king the size of a toddler. Forty pounds, Clem guesses. It takes two hands to haul it in. I think of my mom. When will they tell my sister about me? Will they at all?

Puke and waves. My own smallness. Time to think or not to think, to have a sister or not have a sister, fourteen hours in the troll pit, bracing against the rail, feeling the speed all drain out of me, and eventually, Clem breaks the silence.

"First day of fishing," he says. "How's it feel?"

So far it feels like a lot. It feels like the ocean. The ocean, the sea, whatever it is, it's everywhere: all around but somehow also inside me. I feel like a fluid. My knees get splashy when I walk across the deck. The waves move through my guts and when a chop claps the hull, I feel this gotta-shit pulsing in my intestines. That might be the fear. It's the survival suit that has me geeked out. Clem made me practice putting it on last night, at anchor. He timed me with a watch.

"Dead," he said. "Four minutes."

"Dead," he said. "Three minutes."

"Maybe," he said the third time. "Just maybe."

But I tell him fishing feels good. I tell him I'd like to hear more about my dad, but he says no. He brought me out here to work, and that's what we're going to do.

Ten

The engine shaking, and I'm up.

We're anchored in a cove. It's low tide and the passage to the open water is narrow. There are bugs in the cabin, a swarm of little black flies, and under the smell of breakfast there's that briny low-tide seaweed stink. Clem's drinking coffee and Beaver's standing at the bow, growling at some deer on the beach. Fingers of fog comb the pine trees on the mountains. These are the pictures he painted for me, the ones I saved somewhere so deep they can't be deleted. But maybe I don't have to. I meet them head on. I tell them Eat Shit. I out-beauty those old stories with memories of my own and then we motor three miles out, to fish.

With two-foot swells, the sea's a log with a bird on top. A log with three birds on top. A tentacle of bullwhip kelp that could wrap around a house. A group of jellyfish like plastic grocery bags. Or maybe those were just grocery bags. An old buoy. (What is Bonnie doing right this moment?) The nose of a seal. A whale blowing in the distance. The flashers like beer cans in the water. Salmon writhing on the top lines. Mountains, far white cliffs, charter boats, an even smaller smallness and the comfort in that.

I run the lines, catch a few fish.

I run the lines, catch a few fish.

Gaff, bleed, gill, gut. Skeins of roe laced with ropey purple veins. I find a salmon with a smaller salmon in its belly, I forgive my mom, hope she forgives me, and at the bottom of the set, I pull a line and the lure's missing. Below that, the hook's bent straight. Below that, a salmon head with no body. And I used to be squeamish. Look at me now, viscera in my hair, punctures in my hand. It's hard to say whether Pritchard would be disappointed with me. I wrote him a letter after making it through freshman year at G State, and all he'd replied with was a postcard that said, "Well Done, G. Onward," and a long dash that resembled this exact straightened hook.

"Clem."

I hold up the fish head with the tendrils of meat all twisted around each other like DNA.

"That the only one?"

"Some of the hooks are all fucked up. I think I saw a seal earlier."

"No," Clem says. "You saw a sea lion. You saw a sea lion robbing our picnic basket."

"Should I pull the lines?"

"No," he says. He disappears into the cabin and goes below deck and I can hear him rummaging in the closet. When he returns, he has a rifle in his hand.

"Ears," he says, but he doesn't wait.

Pop, pop, pop!

Pop, pop, pop!

Pop, pop, pop!

The sea eats up the bullets.

After he's finished Clem says that one time he handed my dad that same gun and in a remarkable case of misunderstanding, my dad thought the goal was to kill the sea lion, and did. Sea lions are endangered. And buoyant. There were lots of boats on the water. They pulled the lines and motored for two hours just to get away from the scene of the crime.

"Any other deckhand," Clem says, "I would have fired him on the spot."

"Jen told me you really liked my dad."

"He was the best deckhand I ever had."

I gaff a big coho. Bonk it, bleed it. Gill it, gut it. Coffee.

"What did you like about him?"

"He was the best deckhand I ever had."

I rip the gills and the tail slaps blood onto my face.

"She told me you adored him."

He cleans fish like the Native women in Klak, more feel than sight. Three cuts are all it takes. Twenty seconds, tops. When it's done, the fish looks like it never had anything inside of it. Like it was born empty. He says, "Other than my cats and Jen when she was real small, I don't think I've ever adored anything in my life. But your father was probably the only man Jen ever got with that I didn't hate. He had those Hawaii tuna dreams, but really he was here long-term, which meant Jen was here long-term. She'd lived down South for a long time, so it wasn't a hell of a lot more complicated than that."

He starts on another salmon. "I never liked the tuna idea, but I'm old. Everybody's trying to pivot to tuna to make ends meet. But hey, there will still be kings to catch by the time I want to retire."

I say, "They said it was a record in Bristol Bay."

"Yeah. I saw that. Here it's the opposite. Logging, dams, global warming. We still got pinks, but all the coho and especially the kings are going the way of Oregon and Washington. They used to have runs like this. In Canada now, they're paying trollers to retire. Half of the guys I know here under forty are trying to get out. I wish it was different but, hey, what can you do?"

"Wish in one hand, shit in the other."

"Your dad used to always say that. He was a pretty funny guy. One time, he had this camcorder he'd borrowed, and he got this idea. We took a dozen coho that had already been cleaned, put them back on hooks and ran the lines down into the water. Then he hit play and filmed me reeling in these perfect, grocery store looking fish. No guts or anything. They showed the tape in Goldie's for like a year. You got to wonder how many of the people who can afford salmon thinks it come out of the water looking that way."

"Why do you think my dad never told anybody he bailed on us?"

He cracks the gurdy with the back of his hand and the lines drop.

"It's so bright. We need to run the lines deeper."

I drop my lines deeper. I say, "I think it's a fair question to ask."

"I'm done," he says. "Pull the lines."

Eleven

We motor back through Sitka Sound until I see the town's bridges sharpening in the mist and I wonder if Clem's gotten sick of me, tired of my bullshit, fed up with my questions and puke. But he surprises me. He says I need to take Beaver.

"He's got too much energy for me," he says. "And he's always harassing my cats."

"I don't know, Clem," I say. "I've never even had a dog."

"I'm not asking," he says. "I'll pay the pet fee on the plane when you decide to go home."

Right now my mom's probably painting the walls of the spare room pink. Probably telling ladies at the grocery store how I'm off fighting terrorism. I tell Clem I'll take the dog, but I'm not going home. I'm gonna try to get a job sliming at the co-op.

He just nods. He nods a lot. He punches in new coordinates on the GPS.

He says, "Hey what's the difference between a bucket of shit and a slime liner?"

"The bucket. Oh, so this seal walks into a bar."

326 / JAKE MAYNARD

He just waves at me and says he knows them all.

"How about the three fishermen who—"

"All of them."

An hour passes and the cabin's hot and loud from the engine bucking underneath. I pull my hat down over my eyes and somewhere inside of sleep another one comes to me. Bonnie and I were working on nets in the shack and the rain was creeping across the roof and she said, "Hey, what's the difference between jam and jelly?"

I said, "Maybe something to do with the seeds."

She started giggling. She tried to speak, couldn't. Her face turned red. Something girlish about her I hadn't noticed before. The sound of her laughing filled me up and then I started too. It was contagious. I'm starting to think most things are.

"What's so funny?"

"The difference," she said. She paused to gulp some breath. She just couldn't say it.

"What?!"

"The difference is that I can't jelly my dick up your ass."

That's Bonnie Kohle to me. Maybe not to everyone, but to me. I know I barely know her, but maybe that's what made it work. There's this spooky honesty you can get with strangers, the shadow-truth you make out of lies. Maybe that's why she liked me too.

An idea or maybe a dream is coming to me—

"No sleeping," Clem says.

"I fucking wasn't."

"I heard you snoring."

We're not in Sitka. We're motoring through a straight, steep hills on each side thick with spruce. I check the chart on the screen and see we're headed back out to sea. Clem's got the window cracked and I can smell the land disappearing, that clean start-over smell. The straight empties into the bay and I see the open water—gray, it's always gray—and Clem cranks the wheel and the boat cuts across the running tide, bouncing now, the throb in my stomach, toward a little river on the other side.

"Since you're staying," he says. "I got something to show you."

It's not a river, but a cove. It opens up like a secret. The water's green. The trees are green. The rocks are green with green moss and black kelp drying at the tide line. It's all the shades of green, like there was only one color to paint it. A half a mile of that, cutting a long gash through the glassy water behind us, until we find a gravel bar where a little creek dumps into the cove at the headlands. Is this the place? I can feel it—no, him—breathing on my neck.

I say, "This is where you spread the ashes, isn't it?"

"What?" Clem says. "We did that at the cape. This's a different thing altogether."

He drops anchor fifty yards from shore where there's some cleared land with the leftovers of an old dock tilting like a broken jaw. Behind it, a rusted-out truck with a tree growing through the frame. Clem says this is what he wants to show me. He tells me to get the raft and by the time I have it untied from the cabin roof and dropped into the water, he's got a shotgun and some beers ready to go. We paddle to shore and Beaver swims. He hits land before us, running mad circles around the old building foundations. Head down, nose at work. I've never seen him running loose before. This is the real him and he's beautiful.

Clem says, "What do you think?"

"About what?"

"You like canneries so fucking much, here you go. Alaska Packing Co., Bear Cove Facility. I used to sell fish here with my dad when I was a kid. There was a shitload of little canneries back before we had good freezers. Back before good ice machines, even. Another one up in Pelican, another one in Hoonah, about a dozen between here and Ketchikan."

Behind the old pilings exposed by the tide, there's a naked patch of land just above the tide line. It's square. Clem scrapes away some dirt with his boot. Concrete—cracked and buckled, saplings fighting through. He says that was the foundation of the main cannery and it stretched out to a pier. Canning equipment's bulldozed into a pile at one end. Old steam canners rusted away to the frames. Sorting lines crumpled, conveyors tipped over, alders growing through.

He says, "When I was a kid this place was hiring mostly Native women and Filipinos and a few poor white kids from Sitka. Jen's mother worked here for a season when she was about sixteen. There was this supervisor son of a bitch who wouldn't stop playing grab ass with her, so the Filipina girls all locked him in the shitter and piped in a bunch of canning smoke. Almost killed him. She loved to tell that story. Her whole life, she talked about it. She remembered those girls' names. Every time I got on some tough guy shit, she put me in my place with stories like that."

Beaver darts by with a rotting gull in his mouth. When he shakes it, the wings flap like it's trying to fly away.

"He allowed to do that?"

"Your dog," he says, shrugging.

"Shit like this never interested your dad," he says. "He had an Alaska in his head and he was gonna live in it. I used to always remind him Jack London was a communist just to piss him off. Anyway, Jen wanted to bring you out here but then she asked me to do it. She's really struggling with everything."

"How about you?"

He says, "With your dad? Somebody like him, it's easy to feel like the person he could've been died, too. I think that's how Jen sees it. Personally, I don't think there was a better man in there. Still, I get it. It kind of feel like you got robbed of something, don't it?"

"So you try to get it back."

"And next thing you know, you're just chewing holes in the world trying."

I laugh, because it was me biting the fillets.

I laugh, because everything still feels so raw.

"I'm going to tell you something cause I'm tired of holding onto it, but if you tell my daughter, I'm gonna take you out here and leave you on a rock that covers."

He's always saying that thing about a rock that covers.

"Your father, asshole that he was, told me about you and your mother. One night on the boat I was drinking and riding his ass about working the gillnetters' strike in Bristol Bay. I had a hard time letting that go. If I'd known when I met him, he never would've set foot on my boat. Then somehow it just came out, like if he gave me something worse, I'd forgive him for the other thing."

"What'd he say?"

"He just told me was all. I asked if he was ever going to look you up or tell Jen or anything, and he said Nope. Never. I thought about telling her myself but a week went by, then a month. It just got to be too late. Who do you think looked up your mother in the first place? Then you tell me about quitting school and running up here, and I'm wondering if I should've just let it die with him."

"I never wanted to be in school anyway. I just never had an excuse to quit."

"Well, it doesn't matter to me one way or the other what you decide to do next. With your dad, there's not much else to know, other than the fact he's dead."

"Somebody else told me something similar back in June."

"You should have listened to him."

"Her," I say. "Should've listened to her."

That night I take my sleeping bag onto the deck and I lay on a rope coil with the dog curled next to me, and I shiver in the huge, brain-splitting calm, listening to the sea and the rigging chiming and the throbbing in my hand, rising up through my arm, my shoulder, my ears. It's draining clear now, at least, and Clem says that means it's healing. He stared at me for a long time after he said it, hoping I'd get his little analogy or whatever, but I played dumb. Maybe tomorrow or the day after I'll say something like, "I finally understand that thing you said about letting things drain." But not tonight. It's better to be underestimated, right? Besides, I'm not laying here thinking about letting the hurt drain out of me because *trying* to think about it isn't any better than trying not to think about it. But there is one last big question I got. This motherfucking sea. What's the word for the sound it makes? I've been wondering for days. It's the most familiar sound, like something I know from Laurel Lane but can't quite place.

Moaning, whispering, chanting—all the words I come up with sound so human, which makes sense, because maybe the sea's just trying to sound like us, pleading in a way we might understand. Saying chill or slow down or maybe, just, Feel. What I mean is I've been saying *look* when I should've been saying—

"You look pretty goddamned morose," Clem says. He's leaning out the Dutch door with a big glass of wine in his hand.

"I'm trying to figure out the word for that sound the sea makes."

He shrugs, disappears into the cabin.

The word isn't grief, but it's close.

No, Wait!

You know what boat stands for, don't you?

Break Out Another Thousand.

Hey Garrett,

Sorry I missed your emails. I'm back in Portland finally, getting settled after the season. I wish I had all the details for you, but yeah, some wild shit went down after you left. First, Bonnie Kohle got arrested on suspicion of blowing that hose up on the beach and the electric thing. Maybe the house fire, too? It was hard to ever get the whole story so I just stopped trying. She was running around for a couple weeks claiming it was all a set-up, acting real conspiratorial, then all at once the whole thing went away and it turns out she sold the land to Kevin for cheap and just split. Someone else was already working in her shack when I left. I also heard that Klak Fancy lost the Thornrose Contract and now the expansion plans are on hold anyway. Wouldn't surprise me if he sells. Neptune's been hovering over him for years.

Also . . . I haven't told anybody yet, but this was my last year in the industry. IDK if the job's changed or if I have, but I'm just ready to make a move. I'm going back to school to be a science teacher. Following in my mom's footsteps after all, I guess! As far as meeting up in Portland or something, that's not the best idea. That whole Klak part of my life is over.

Good luck with the troller project! You're a gutsy fucker, if nothing else—

Helen.

One

Low light snapped by the cold and the snow blowing sideways across the docks. Shore birds have peace'd, bears asleep, Beaver on deck, trying to murder his own tail. Sunday, my day off from the co-op, and I'm tiptoeing around the boat parts and repair manuals and paperwork and library books scattered around the cabin, wondering where to start. The radio's playing old country. Grease left on the dial when I turn it down. Grease on the phone keys, too. Static, ringing—

"What?!"

"Hey Bonnie, it's me. Heard you might be looking for a job."

Acknowledgments

Publishing a book takes all hands on deck. Many thanks to the crew of the F/V Slime—

My agent, Martha Wydysh.
Sarah Munroe, Derek Krissoff, Than Saffel, and the team at West Virginia University Press.
Captain Dan Brigham of the F/V Steadfast.
My old friends from Homer, especially the seaside farmers.
My writing teachers and friends from Hiram College and WVU.
Noelle Mateer.
Natalie and John Maynard, for their life lessons in empathy and solidarity.